HYDROPLANE

HYDROPLANE

SUSAN STEINBERG

NORMAL/TALLAHASSEE

Published by FC2 with support provided by Florida State University,
the Publications Unit of the Department of English at Illinois State
University, and the Florida Arts Council of the Florida Division of
Cultural Affairs. This project is supported in part by an award from
the National Endowment for the Arts, which believes that a great
nation deserves great art.

Address all inquiries to: Fiction Collective Two, Florida State University,
c/o English Department, Tallahassee, FL 32306-1580

ISBN-10: Paper, 1-57366-129-5
ISBN-13 Paper, 978-1-57366-129-4

Library of Congress Cataloging-in-Publication Data
Steinberg, Susan.
  Hydroplane / by Susan Steinberg.— 1st ed.
     p. cm.
  Short stories.
  ISBN 1-57366-129-5 (pbk.)
  I. Title.
  PS3619.T4762H93 2006
  813'.6—dc22

                                    2005036138

Cover Design: Lou Robinson
Book Design: Jane Carman and Tara Reeser

Produced and printed in the United States of America
Printed on recycled paper with soy ink

ACKNOWLEDGEMENTS

Several stories from this collection were first accepted elsewhere
in various forms:

"Lifelike," "The Last Guest," and "Hydroplane" in *Conjunctions*
"Caught" in *Columbia: A Journal of Literature and Art*
"Souvenir" and "The Walk" in *Denver Quarterly*
"Invitation" in *Alaska Quarterly Review*
"To Sit, Unmoving" in *McSweeney's*
"The Garage" in *Boulevard*
"Court" in *American Short Fiction*

I wish to thank John Edgar Wideman, Noy Holland, Lynne Layton, Nicholas Montemarano, K. R. Mogensen, Andrew Altschul, Yaddo, The MacDowell Colony, the University of Massachusetts Amherst, Central Missouri State University, and the University of San Francisco.

CONTENTS

Lifelike

The start. There were fits. Then fitful thoughts. But first there were stars. They flashed past my face. And I watched them flash. And I felt my pulse. And the speed. I need not say.

I was at school. We were critiquing. We stood to look at the paintings. They were green and brown, I recall. Of course. They were trees and trees are green and brown. Whether or not the paintings were good. No matter. The teacher was saying words on them. The girl whose paintings they were said words. I can't recall what either said. Something of harmony. Or something of truth. Nothing significant. I should know. I too was a painter who painted trees. I painted faces. And I painted because I was good at painting. I could make a tree look like a tree. A face look like a face. The teachers often looked over my shoulders. Often they said, nice tree. But what of a tree looking facelike in life. As often they did. We were driving when I caught the trees looking at me. My boyfriend drove. He said, you need help. But the trees had ancient faces. Like mine would become. Made of bark and lined. So help me, I said. Ha ha. He laughed too.

How the fits started I can't say. There was a trigger-point perhaps. Some trigger-point I can't recall. A spark. I can't recall. I listened close to the words of the girl. I listened too to the teacher's. I stood for a closer look at the paintings. The teacher said, a break. And as I took a step to the door I stopped. A piece of time must have passed. A beat. Then there were stars by my head. There were stars too inside. My head that is. And more time passed. And the room thinned quickly to a tube. I was looking through one end of the tube. And everyone else was stuck inside it. They were trying to crawl through its other side. There was light on that side. And inside light shot past like stars. My pulse was speeding with the light. I can't explain it better. I turned to the person nearest me. It was the teacher curved as a letter S. He would help, I knew. I said, I don't feel well. He shrugged or laughed or said, what can I do. I said, help me. I clutched his arm. He said, what's wrong. I said, I don't know, and he said, well, what's wrong. Well, my pulse was speeding. And light shot past like stars.

Everything of course shifted at that point as things shift. Meaning once it shifted it stayed as such. I saw everything through the narrow tube. This isn't symbolic, this weightless invisible tube. Through it were the trees, my hands, the clouds. And through it things near blurred from recognition. Things far loomed and shadowed. I really can't explain it better. How the fits swam under my skin. I could feel them as the swimmer would. I felt them too as water.

I saw no good reason to leave the house. My boyfriend tried to make me laugh. I took pills when I had to leave. I only left to get the mail. I took pills too in the house. They made me feel like a rain-soaked shirt. And the tube went limp. Slack. It disintegrated into. You know. Nothing. The teachers called when I missed those weeks. My boyfriend answered the phone for me. He talked to the teachers in whispers. I heard my boyfriend laughing. I don't know what he told them. I think that I was sick. I talked into the sheets when he wasn't looking. Sometimes words of no significance. Like those. At some point I stopped taking the pills. They were making me hateful and I didn't want to hate. My boyfriend danced to make me laugh. My mother said to take the pills damn it. She said, get some sleep. My boyfriend took the pills away. He said, you need to eat. But the food on my plate had turned too lifelike. The green and brown were the same as life, all landing on the floor when I threw the plate.

The teacher said, what's wrong. Well, for one he was S-shaped. For two he was curved inside the tube. And my pulse. My God. He said, well, what's wrong. It must sound like nothing how I explain it. But trust me it was frantic. I clutched his shirt front. Then his arm. It was hotter than you'd think. I can't recall what he said or did then. But I know he didn't help. I ran from the classroom to the basement. In the basement I found nothing. Then a light. A phone. The tube thinned. I called my mother. She rushed to get me. I waited outside under a car. Imagine her face when I crawled out from under. She wore diamond rings. My face was smudged. She drove me to the doctor. She never liked my boyfriend. Inside her car was freezing. The doctor said, hold still. I was hiding under the paper sheet shaking. My boyfriend couldn't be bothered that day. And my mother, how she carried on.

Needless to say, I had fitful thoughts. Nothing significant. Thoughts on truth as we have and we have them. How you strike a match and the fire goes out. But first the cigarette lights. Life, you think and you have this thought. One thing rubs against another. Something else gains a spark. Then the cigarette is crushed under a heel. Like that.

And there were thoughts on trees. They often looked too vegetal. Like overgrown broccoli stalks. I could see no difference between trees and broccoli. Except the size. And except their ancient faces, the trees. They often looked so animal.

I lied to you. It wasn't my mother who picked me up when I ran to the basement. It was my boyfriend. I called my mother first. She answered the phone. But she couldn't talk long that day, I recall. She had things in her life. Significant things. So my boyfriend came to get me. I waited under a car. He laughed when I crawled out from under. My face was smudged. He drove me to the doctor. He hated my mother. He said she was always pushing. I was sweating sitting in his car. The trees were looking at me funny. The clouds as well. And they never stay still, the clouds. Even when it seems they are. The trees were looking through ancient eyes. And mine would one day too turn ancient. Slits in folds of hardened fat. My boyfriend said, I can't drive any faster. I left my boyfriend in his car. He drove beside me. He told me, get in. I ran and my pulse went faster. I ran up an alley where he couldn't drive. I pressed my pulse to slow the speed. I sat near a pile of dirty leaves. My mother wanted things for me. Marriage. Money. Only the best. My boyfriend's car went past. It was rusted at the bottom. He didn't see me in the gutter. The leaves made a sound. Like what. Like static. And the light changed. Meaning the sun set. It was pink at first, the light. Divine. The traffic thinned to nothing.

I recall late one night I left the house. I couldn't sleep so thought to paint at school. The girl from class was painting too. I hadn't been to class in weeks. She never asked me why. I should say there was a wall between us. This isn't symbolic. There was a literal wall. And from her wall side she talked and I talked back. And we were having a pretty good talk. We talked about painting and school and the teacher. Really nothing significant. But we got to laughing hard. Then she came to my space on my wall side. And this was friendship, I decided. Laughing hard over nothing and talking. And half a beat after I decided friendship was in fact a fixed thing. So for half a beat after my decision I felt fit. I wanted to squeeze this girl on my wall side. But then I recalled friendship wasn't fixed. How could it be when trees were far bigger and rooted in dirt and yet trees weren't fixed. And how when diamonds were hard and sharp enough to cut glass and yet not fixed. I knew about clouds. I knew they were over you one second and over someone else the next. I knew they too were often dark and swollen with rain. And I knew all our laughing and talking would be caught in the clouds and taken somewhere at cloud speed.

I rose from the gutter. I ran to the doctor. My boyfriend met me there. The doctor said, hold still. Boy did I shake under the sheet. My boyfriend was sweating. My mother couldn't be bothered that day. There was shopping of sorts. She had friends. Good ones. Driving home my boyfriend said, that cunt.

I said to my boyfriend, you can be with whomever. I said, it doesn't matter. I said, get out of my face. Please, I said. I said, please just be with someone else. It didn't matter. He didn't get me. He was always smoking by my mailbox. And he drank at night. It was never enough to pass him out. He answered the phone when I told him not to. Then it was he and the teachers using words. He and my mother fighting. But no one knew what was best for me. And I didn't know. I knew we weren't to be fixed, he and I. He saw trees as trees and that was a laugh. There was nothing fixed besides. He was poor besides. My mother said I should look a bit harder. But trust me I was looking. I looked so hard I couldn't get near him. It wasn't his fault. He had turned too lifelike. Across the room he loomed and shadowed the room. Up near he pushed and blurred in my face like food. I said, get out of my face. He went soft. Slack. I thought, how sad. Like an old sleeping animal. An overcooked vegetable.

It occurred to me in my boyfriend's car that paintings do depict life. I thought, yes. I thought, paintings are unfixed as life. Of course. My mother's diamonds always flashed in the sunlight. The sun burned white in her black glasses. And in her hair. And I knew the sun would fade her hair. It would yellow her diamonds. Her face was turning lined and hard as bark. And I knew the sun would also fade. I knew the earth would turn cold. The air was ice in my mother's car. My boyfriend kept his windows down. For air, he said. I left his car. I ran to the doctor. The doctor said, take these.

We could have formed a friendship that night me and the girl. We were laughing so hard and talking. But I was thinking. And my laughing stopped. And her laughing stopped for a second. She was taking a break. Just one second. She held up one finger. Just two seconds. Just to get her cigarette lit. She struck the match. She took a long drag off her cigarette. And I saw no smoke float from

her after the drag. This isn't to say she wasn't breathing. She was.
She was even talking again. But I watched as she dragged long and
no smoke floated from her mouth. Nor from her nose. I thought
there must be something wrong. I thought, she can't go on like
this. I stood nearer. I watched the cigarette tip brighten and saw no
smoke float from her face. I stood with my side pressed to her side.
I whispered, what on earth. She said, what's wrong with you. The
room was starting up. My pulse. I whispered, my God. She backed
away. She walked back to her side. I followed her. She said, stop.

Earlier that day my mother had sent me flowers. This isn't
symbolic. They were right by the mailbox. Then she called. She
told my boyfriend, they'll brighten the room. They'll fix things,
she said. The flowers were very bright. But the petals were already
drying. Some had fallen to the floor. So there they were, scattered.
There's nothing deeper to this.

My boyfriend called. He broke up with me. It wasn't his fault.
He said, sorry. No matter. I threw my plate. I felt I was supposed to.
All those broken bits. Those greens and browns. All that food was
once life growing. In fields. And the sun shone over and brightened
the fields. Then something crushed the animals. Then everything
green was crushed as well. And there it was on my kitchen floor.
What's that, you say. I say, your guess. I could have dropped to my
knees. I admit I felt unfit.

It was wrong from the start. We met at a dinner. My mother
looked at his shirt. Torn. He looked at her diamonds. She looked
at my hair. I looked at her face. She looked at the paint on my
clothes. There wasn't much to say except pass this pass that. I
sensed the first flicker of stars. Off to the sides by my ears. Passed
off as drunken, I'm guessing. I had been drinking. Some air, I said.

I left to sit on the curb. Cars went past. I pushed leaves in the gutter with my hands. What they said in my absence. Well, there was a fight. I saw my boyfriend huff to his rusted car. I saw my mother follow, smirking smugly. I left too.

I recall the critique. The paintings were awful. The colors. Awful dirty greens. The teacher was spitting out words that day. The girl was carrying on. She said something of truth and harmony. It was really quite funny and the teacher said, break. I looked at her paintings. I looked good and hard at the mess. Her truth. I laughed good and hard. The teacher looked up. The girl looked hurt. What was that. The trigger. That shallow cunt. I hated her paintings. Her poor hurt face. I said, help.

The first fit hit me like a fist in the mouth. My mother's, that is. Diamonds square in the face. The next fits were softer. Expected. Like her smirking and handing a hairbrush saying, brush it. Or a white dress saying, try it. Or a bar of soap saying, paint on your hands. Your clothes. Your face. Or a diamond smirking, one day it's yours. Your father gave it to me that son of a bitch. And when I flinch she hands a twenty. A hundred. To take off the edge.

My mother couldn't get me from school. She had shopping or some such. She had very good friends. I was shaking hard. She knew I was shaking. I was having thoughts. The tube as a tunnel. The light at the end. You've heard it before. The teacher came down looking for me. The girl came down with the teacher. My things were up in the classroom. The girl and the teacher were calling my name. Their voices pushed like spreading roots that tore up the basement floor. And before they could reach me I was running outside. I was crawling under a car. I was hiding from the mess. I was looking for my mother. But my boyfriend's car went past.

When the flowers lost their petals. Well, I thought, now this is fixed. Not the shell shapes. Not the dry veins I could see with light. But that they would disintegrate as they do. That they would turn to nothing. That was fixed. I know you've thought this. Who hasn't thought it. But I hadn't yet. And this is mine.

The way she handed a brush to fix my hair. I said, stop it. She dragged it through my hair. It made a sound I can't explain. You're thinking, sparks. Something sparking. Yes. She said, your look. She shook her head. Her fist made contact with her palm. Never my face. But she meant it. To strike it. I saw lights in her diamonds. Her car was ice. She gripped the wheel. You just need two things, she always said. Marriage and money. My mother got both. But both were unfixed. Her glasses had the blackest lenses. I couldn't tell you of her eyes. I must admit. Only my father's diamond was real. The rest were glass. My boyfriend smoked down to the fingers. When I say I loved him. Well, what do you think. He pointed to trees and clouds. He said, looks good to me. I know what you're thinking. But was there a spark.

When my mother called I hid in the sheets. It's my mother, I said to my boyfriend. Yes mother, I said to her face. To her voice. That cunt, I said when she wasn't with me. In the mirror that is I said, that cunt. She was with me. I would get old.

What I recall from school. How you often have to squint to see. How you often have to back away. How a tree is a tree and a face a face. And something of the colors brown and green. And something of trees being brown and green. And something of the colors black and white. And of black being the presence of all colors. No that's light. White. Black being the absence of all colors.

I can't recall. And something of harmony, something of truth. I can't recall. No matter.

I lied to you. My mother had brought the flowers. I went for the mail. And there she stood by the mailbox. She was looking old. She had food on her face. She said, you're looking fit, and looked away. My boyfriend was smoking. I said to him, go. I meant for him to. But she handed the flowers to my boyfriend. She said, they'll brighten the room. Then she started to leave. I said, you stay Mother. I pushed my boyfriend. I said, please get out of my face. He held the flowers in front of his head. My mother said, come. We went shopping. We bought nothing. When I got home my boyfriend was gone. I was somewhat on edge. My mother had tried to fix me up. With clothes and the rest. With boyfriends. Imagine. The fight in the car. I need not say. At home the petals were scattered. My boyfriend called. He said, let's break up. I said, okay. I threw the plate. The flowers.

And I went to school that night. The girl and I laughed. We talked of nothing significant. And I thought of friendship. I thought of me and the girl as friends. And she smoked and swallowed the smoke.

And I thought of trees. How they grow out of nothing. Dirt. How they grow into nothing. Air. How somehow there's life. A spark. Until it gets crushed. That's life you know. Screaming oneself awake. Redfaced and bald. Closing the eyes. Bald again. Just stop me now. I knew nothing. I admit it. I know nothing.

The girl. I tried to tell her. I had nothing to tell. But I tried. I pushed against her. I said, what on earth. I was starting up. She said, what's wrong with you, and walked away. I followed her into her space. I looked at her paintings. I would say sorry for laughing in class. Sorry for being so unfit. She looked so hurt. She said, stop. I thought, sorry for laughing. But her paintings were spread across her wall. And they were awful. Lifelike one could say. I felt I would laugh into fits. I knew she would hurt when I did. And I started to laugh. But I wasn't laughing. I felt it starting. I said, I don't feel well. Stop, she said.

In the end I saw the girl through the tube. She looked scared. Or hurt. She looked far away. And light shot past like stars. I went outside. I went under a car. My pulse began to slow. At some point the sun rose and shone over top. It brightened the gutter. The leaves in the gutter were bright. This isn't symbolic. I didn't think of my boyfriend. I didn't think of my mother. I didn't cry into the leaves for goodness sake. I just breathed as we do.

Souvenir

It was him on my way to the market. There were things I needed. Milk. Bread. But he stood for the bus in a crowd. In rain. I stopped.

It was him I knew in the narrow nose. In the filmy cheeks and hair. Even the sweater looked his. The diamond shapes. And the fisherman's cap. I knew it too well. Always kept with the others on the closet shelf. Over his ladyfriend's Russian furs.

I swayed for a second. I wouldn't say reeled but I felt as my legs gave way.

He was swaying too a bit it seemed. But no he wasn't. Just it was windy, turning more than a drizzle.

Others stood with umbrellas. They wore raincoats. They

looked to me, then to their shoes.

His jacket was shoddy. Last year's outdated. It was strange to see his exhale. I wouldn't say painful. Just the last time I saw him he had been gasping.

And when he turned to me now. Split second. Well, I clutched the bus stop signpost tight from the curb. The others knew not to look at me. They watched for the bus.

I was a fool, I knew it. I felt like one. But I hadn't seen that posture in two plus years. I had near forgotten that diamond sweater. Those scuffed brown shoes. Thin clouds on the exhale.

He looked again.

And had he said word one to me. Even, what time do you have. Well, I was trying my damnedest not to flat-out faint. I just needed to get to the market. It would close soon. There were things I wanted. Bread.

Plus the rain was falling harder. I should have driven. I turned to walk.

But I had so much to say. A lot had gone on.

For one small thing the bus fare. A whole new cost.

For another my plants had grown to this long.

And my car. Older but fine. Just one breakdown in the two plus years. A jump-start and it worked good as new. And the wipers sometimes shut off. Unexpected. Almost always during a big storm. Go figure.

A good reason to walk or take the bus.

He would have laughed at this.

And my cat was still going. Twelve years and counting. He sleeps most days, I wanted to say.

There was my job.

Various places closed down in the city. Various opened.

And the Orioles still were no good lousy. We could all agree. Those slobs.

When he looked again I thought to speak. Or to grab hold of his sweater.

His hair moved around his cap edge. He needed a shave. An umbrella. A raincoat. He needed the bus already. Where was it.

It's funny. I never remembered him taking the bus. He owned a two-toned car the last year. Blue and light blue. Sporty, he said of it.

But you can't take it with you is how it goes. The car was sold to a neighbor. A stranger. Mister so-and-so from two doors down. And the furniture too. And the other things I wanted. His paintings for instance. He was a painter. And the forks were sold off. All of the silver in fact. But the forks somehow stood out as significant. I wouldn't say sacred. Just all those dinners at his house.

I tried to keep a fork but my father shook it from my hand.

They're a set, he said. It clattered to the floor.

I wanted the two-toned car but I had a car.

For awhile we watched TV. Me and my father. It was something funny. Then it turned serious. He pulled the plug. He took the TV to the neighbor's.

I sat in quiet.

So much to say and the bus was coming.

I was curious, had he seen anyone else from the family. Or anyone famous. And where had he been anyway all this time. I wasn't thinking foreign countries. I wasn't thinking heaven or hell. I wasn't like that. All that nonsense talk of clouds and fire. The rabbi's words. And why not in a closet, I wanted to ask. Hiding in his ladyfriend's battered furs. In a pocket with her scented lipsticks.

Or more absurd.

Like clinging to my father's earlobe. Whispering, you'll never amount. You bum.

But he always said you die you rot.

I never believed it.

You evaporate.

No. Not true.

I knew it was him with that stubborn posture never swaying in the downpour. I knew his downward look. His bitterness. That scowl, I knew it well.

It said, you never saved me, you fool.

He wanted to live.

Well, who doesn't. It's funny.

Everyone knew the doctors made a mistake. They shouldn't have cut him open. He was getting old. Getting weak. But he wasn't so sick. So they said. He could've recovered with no procedure. They said this to my father.

My father said, go for it.

When he flat-lined his ladyfriend said, someone goofed. She cursed in Russian.

It rained that day too. It always seems to when it should.

My father planned a service quick. The following day he spoke. There were rows of flowers. Bowls of bitter Russian candies. The rabbi talking of clouds. Of doves. The desert and fire. My father didn't cry for his father. No one did.

And two plus years later I sure wasn't crying. I was thinking of wearing his shoes in the rain. Strange as that was. I was thinking of feeling the hot leather insides. I used to wear them and clomp through his hallways. The brown ones looked more like girl shoes. But I could fit both feet inside one if I wanted.

I sat in his chair in his shoes before dinner. I could fit my whole body in one corner of the chair. I slept in the corner and the shoes slipped off.

Then we ate.

When the line flattened the predictable tone followed. Like watching serious TV, said my father. And we'd seen so much TV we knew just how to act. Either courageous or sobbing.

We were courageous. Even laughing.

We even went to the gift shop to browse. We even went to the cafeteria. The game was on. My father managed a, go!

Those slobs.

Those fools, I said.

I never saw it coming.

Well, no one did. Those show-off doctors. Someone goofed.

His ladyfriend cursed her head off in Russian. It was the damnedest time trying to shut her off.

It's natural.

He's still with us.

Eat your pie.

Good girl.

No one knew what my father was saying. I said not one word but whistled instead. Maybe for the first time ever. My father said, stop that lousy whistling.

But I couldn't stop at first. Then I laughed so hard I had to leave. I wandered the hallways and stood in the stairwell. I laughed in the lousy stairwell lighting. There were echoes.

The Orioles would have won that day. But the rain.

I left without a word.

I sat in the breakdown lane when my wipers shut off. And I didn't cry but it seemed I was. All those rainstreak shadows on my skin.

I at least felt sad, I admit. Picture the cafeteria's light green walls. The souvenirs they sell in gift shops. My father's shoddy overcoat. Pie crumbs on a smear of lipstick.

The gasping before the solid line.

The filmy eyes saying, save me, you fool.

But it wasn't my job.

Funny how slow I drove when the wipers recovered. Thinking of nothing but gray and gray and gray.

At home was quiet. Then a mouse darted through the hallway and back. Then the cat.

I thought, go for it.

I wasn't surprised by the chase. I almost expected the kill. It was a parallel.

And the mouse too didn't die all the way. Not at first I mean. Picture it. And the cat was already sleeping. I left the mouse in the hallway and slept.

In my dreams I was chased. Not surprising.

I waked when my father called in the morning. He said, don't be late.

Later he spoke. Nothing significant. And the rabbi said, one dies so one lives. I didn't believe him.

Later I talked to my father. I told him of the cat. The parallel.

I said, one dies so another dies.

How the ladyfriend carried on. Her lipstick bleeding to her teeth. Russian candies puffing her face.

She mumbled, what the hell is she talking about.

My father scowled.

I said nothing.

It was odd staying where he had lived. I wouldn't say scary. Just all his things going into boxes. A funny procedure. It went on for days and days.

At some point my father got the ashes. He dumped them in the damnedest place. He said, he deserved it.

Then he laughed.

Well, I couldn't tell this to the man at the bus stop. His stubborn posture would have bent. He would have screamed, that lousy bum! Your father's a bum!

He would have told a story to the crowd.

Here's how her father lost his job.

Here's how her father wrecked his life.

Here's how her father wrecked his kid.

But the ashes blended right into the drive. All that gray. My father backed the two-toned car and drove it two doors down. He carried the furniture alone. The paintings.

His father would have said, you lousy show-off. You'll wreck the paintings.

And after all that time. All that work.

I thought how he once showed me to paint. Outside. In fall. He wore a sweater that day too. A cap. I watched the exhale float from his face. And I wasn't thinking life that day. Just cold. Gray. We painted a tree. The plants around it. He said to use black for the trunk. Green for the leaves.

I used green for the trunk. He scowled.

My father waved from the window. He laughed at my tree.

The ladyfriend brought us bitter candies.

She always kept his furniture polished and more. His silver.

He always said, she's a keeper.

She said, I don't want his things. She packed up hers and went to her son's.

My father boxed the forks. Insignificant after all. He made me stand. He carried the chair on his back to the neighbor's. It was black leather. It was his father's most-liked chair. The one where I slept before dinner. His shoes slipped off when I slept. I no longer fit in a corner. Not surprising.

I took a spoon when my father wasn't looking. I put it in my pocket. A souvenir.

So much to say as the rain fell harder. I had no umbrella.

It was only an old man, you fool. A stranger.

And I needed to get to the market.

I noticed his shoes had come undone. I considered crouching. But he stood proud, letting the laces hover and flop.

Stubborn. Just like him.

His ladyfriend sure would have crouched and tied them. She would have said, you stubborn man.

I wonder now why I stood in the downpour. It was cold out.

I wonder too how he kept his cap. His things. You're not supposed to take it with you. Everyone knows.

It wasn't him, you fool.

I know.

When we finished putting things in boxes I didn't look around. There was nothing but space besides. Boxes. I left his house for the last time ever. My car wouldn't start. It was night. Raining again. The neighbor jumped my car with the two-toned car. Good as new.

Then in the breakdown lane I considered some things. Nothing significant now.

At home I remembered the mouse. It had crawled to a corner and died. I scooped it up with the spoon. I threw it to the street. Spoon and all. It disappeared into the downpour.

And now my hair was drenched.

I had no money for the bus. Just enough for the market.

My cat was old and slow.

My job.

And I was whistling again. He was withering there. I wouldn't say evaporating. But the word came to me.

Then the bus.

Caught

Lord she was glorious in that dress. Fresh, I would venture, brilliant.

And good to see the Chinese wilted flower pattern, perhaps outdated, of black and red on a night so wet. Fastened off-center, as it was, and short, I spied her knees despite my speed through the doorway, and suntanned they were, brilliant, golden.

My mother would have piped in, Cheap, but this girl, she struck me, and I struck her as well, though, funny, with the door is how I did. And she didn't flinch when it smacked her, though I did flinch outright, feeling the smack, then seeing her brilliant, static poise.

She was glorious in that light.

But here's me talking of a girl, of a dress, when I had rushed in rain-soaked, gasping, lord, like a wet dog, as the old saying goes, into the ladies' room, my hair matted flat, my skirt dripping wet as if water sprung from leaks in the skirt itself.

My mother would have said, Dry those clothes, had I shown to her house wet as that. Dry up, she would have said, pitching a towel. She would have said, A drowned rat is what she looks like, and I did look a sight, squeaking wet shoes across the tiles, squeezing water from my hair with paper.

I knew I had to rush—there was no denying—time was flying past.

There was dinner waiting and talk—we had hardly talked all year, I with my life, my mother with hers. There were neighbors waiting, and here I was late, the drive one more hour, at least, and what kind of daughter, yes, yes, I had heard it. I should have called more often, I should have driven quicker; I had heard it all. I would rush.

But I was soaked to the bones, as they say, and drying, not thinking of the reason I had rushed in first, which was to use the room, so to speak. How odd to say, to use.

And I was too soaked to use anything, really, my skirt matted smack to my legs, heavy with wet, and dark.

And this girl stood poised under the heat light, bone-dry, glorious in Chinese flowers, not looking at me, at my burst through the door, but looking only at herself in the mirror.

I would explain my lateness to my mother.

I would tell her weather, Bad weather, I swear.

She would say, She brings bad weather with her, She always has, Am I right.

She would say, The rainclouds must follow her around, all the times she's rushed in soaked from rain.

The neighbors would laugh behind their hands. They would

give the looks that say, We shouldn't be laughing at the poor thing, should we.

And I would explain my look. That weather was to blame. That I dried my rain-soaked hair with paper, I swear, in a tavern, in the ladies'.

My mother would say, She could have stopped off, cleaned up, dried a bit more to be decent, for decency still counts, Am I right, And anything less than decent is not worth the drive.

Tell me if I'm not right.

I went into one stall, the girl into the other, both of us locking, unbuttoning, and sitting, though I never, in general, sat all the way, but here, for some reason, I did and hard. The seat was hot from the heat light, I ventured, so hot I could have slept there and waked in hours, days, when someone happened to knock and wake me. I could have slept there, head to the door.

And I started to drain, my mother's word, more decent, she thought, than piss or pee or whatever we said as kids.

I spied the girl's black slipper under the divider, and I thought how small; my feet would never have fit in shoes so perfect and small, and how curious, too, her shoes, they were dry. In a blinding downpour. How odd.

I thought, did she hear how my big, soaked shoes had squeaked across the tiles on my way to the stall like a bad hinge worn from use. I could have blushed, were I that type, and had she heard my shoes, cheap as they were, squeaking across, and she must have heard, her shoes being so curiously dry; they were slippers; who wouldn't have heard.

Like buffalo, my mother once piped through a smirking mouth. Like a whole herd of buffalo coming through the house, and I laughed with the neighbors. You're funny, I said.

Well, this girl must have been on her way out, and the rain must have rained during her dinner, for she was dry. And I was sure she had already eaten, for she did seem, somehow, already fed, satisfied, it seemed, in the way she took her time.

I slowed my speed to hers.

I thought of her hands, small, propping her up from the seat.

I thought of her face, her gaze on the door of the stall.

And I knew her date waited at the bar, a wiry one, chewing a toothpick, taking a mint for later.

And I could tell they would leave, these two. He would take her somewhere, to a lot, to sit, to kiss; I knew this part, the rush.

There was no denying the heat of hands on the back.

My mother would have said, That animal, had he been mine looking so rough as that, looking him toe to face as he sucked his toothpick waiting for his girl.

My mother would have said, And where does he work, Am I right.

She would have smirked, She had better not bring that one home.

The neighbors would have laughed into their shirts, their knees.

I would never have brought one home.

The neighbors had daughters too.

And the daughters never brought them home.

And if I told the neighbors a thing or more of their daughters. I had spied those nights in summers. I had seen a thing or more.

But I would watch my tongue. I always watched it.

I was decent, I was.

So much so, I thought to tell her to wait—it was storming sideways—and I almost did tell her, looking at her perfect slipper, Wait. But we were in separate stalls, as it was, and I would never have struck up talk.

I was decent.

And surely her date would say, Let's wait; he had brains, sure, and would buy the drinks—for him something cheap in a shot glass, for her something sweet with a cherry. But strong.

She could take it.

I could tell.

And perhaps I would have a drink at the bar with the girl and her date, a shot, perhaps, and quick I would eat; I was starved.

We would clink our drinks, give a toast to life, then laugh at the storm, at the three of us sitting there, caught.

I would leave soon as I could; I would speed. Just one more hour, then dinner, reheated, but I needed to dry before my mother saw me so soaked.

I sat hard, draining, not wanting to rise just yet, and she was beside me, a wall between us, a thin divider, and she drained as well, and drained, it seemed, at the very same pressure, the very same pitch and speed.

Crazy to think such thoughts I thought. But I wasn't one to blush.

I could barely pull up my rain-soaked skirt.

I heard her rise, adjust.

And I wondered of this date outside the door, some wiry steady, I knew he was. He was wiry-fingered, and I wondered of him. Of them. Of what they would do in the lot. I knew of tongues, the taste of mint; I knew nights in lots, hands hot on my back, those wiry ones I loved.

Then barefoot, creeping across the grass, I could see my window. I was golden.

But the neighbors' windows always lighted. Their curtains parted shining squares of light on the grass as I pushed up my window.

Caught.

I always wondered how to fit in.

I almost always found a way.

The neighbors' lights went off. The grass below my window blacked.

And I watched the ceiling from the bed, thought of the night, of the lot, of the wiry one, the rush of him, whoever he was, and I stayed in bed still feeling his hands, still hearing the suck and suck of us.

It was summer.

At night I returned to the lot.

So I knew they were going to sit in a lot, these two, perhaps the one out front.

My car was in that lot, the keys in the car, the motor running. I had so needed to drain the last several miles, I parked and ran, not thinking.

And now I opened the door to the stall, ran water, faced the mirror, faced her face in the mirror.

I would explain her face.

How satisfied.

And I would explain the weather.

It was thought to be drizzling but grew to a downpour, I swear it.

My mother would shake a plate of blackened food below my face, saying, That ungrateful, The dinner was cooked and re-cooked and recooked.

The neighbors would nod their heads, make the faces, then the arms around my mother's back that say, You've worked so hard and she's still good for nothing.

Let her go already.

I would say, Surely I'm good for something.

Surely the neighbors knew I was.

My mother would pitch the plate to the table, storm to her

room, slam the door, crying, dramatic.

I would shake my head, say, That leaky faucet, and laugh alone.

I would wait with the neighbors until dark, until one of them walked me to my car, said, Go.

It was always this.

I was always late.

I was always waiting, then leaving red-faced.

And here I was on my way.

I would stall.

It was glorious with the hum of the fan, the flower soap smell, the sucking sound of the drains. And lord she was tall, I saw, as we soaped our hands in side-by-side sinks under the light.

I would explain her turn of the faucet, the steam in the mirror.

Then she was gone from the mirror, so I turned my faucet.

So it wasn't just me there.

You see.

It never just was.

If I told the neighbors, Look.

It wasn't just me there.

I would tell them, Look.

Those brainless good-for-nothings, and they knew it, the neighbors, their animal daughters I had seen in lots at night.

Take a look at your girls.

I would watch my tongue.

I would watch it go.

Your girls, I would say.

Banged-up knees and brainless.

Sweet they seemed.

Indecent.

I had the rush of hands on my back until late. The girls had hands rushing all the way up and up. And more. I knew. I had spied.

Just they came home early. They were sweet in their dresses. A hello to their mother, the father, a kiss in the air, and everyone went to their rooms.

Just they were animals that way. Rushing through it. Rushing home.

And they didn't sleep but went to their windows, the daughters, their mother, the father, to catch me. They waited for me to walk across grass, to catch me at my window, golden.

Sure, they always caught me.

I almost always fit right in.

But that once I pushed my window up. The neighbors' windows lighted. It rained.

And the rain had tapped the car in the lot; it had streaked the windows. It was warm in the car, getting hot, hotter, then later, and he said he would drive me home. The rain, he said, but I wanted to walk across the grass.

I walked as slowly as I could.

I pushed my window upward.

My mother stood in my lighted square.

Sure, I couldn't fit.

I almost said, Well, look, I can explain.

I almost said, Let me in.

But she pushed the window down on my fingers, hissing, You indecent good-for-nothing.

The neighbors' lights went off. The grass went dark. It rained.

I sat beneath my window, fingers wilted in the grass until the rain stopped, the sun rose, my mother left for work.

Indecent, they whispered behind their hands.

Not me. Their girls.

This time I would say it.

Animals.

Brainless.

And I would run to my car, my mother steaming in the door-way, Where do you think you're going so soon, you ungrateful.

Let her go.

I would drive the way home and never return.

I would say, Look, I've let you go.

I would laugh alone. I'm funny, I would say.

I laughed aloud in the ladies'.

The girl turned off her faucet.

So it was her in the mirror, alone, you see.

So I turned my faucet to be with her.

I felt it when she looked at me.

I can explain her look.

It was good for something.

So I looked back.

But she was gone from the mirror, rushing past me, drying her hands on her Chinese flowers.

She reached for the doorknob and pulled.

I wanted to say, Not yet, Wait.

I wanted to say, The rain.

She left streaks of wet across her dress.

She was gone from the room in a rush.

And I was brilliant, lord, in the mirror.

I was static, poised, drying out in the light.

The Last Guest

The last guest, the redhead, late and standing in the doorway, the door half open so that only half of him is seen before he pushes the door to fully open, as he can do this if he wants, as he can push the door to fully open as he's been invited by the hostess and is, therefore, never needing to knock, but needing only to push the door.

The last guest standing in the doorway, pressing out his cigarette on the vestibule wall, letting the cigarette drop, crushed, in a spray of sparks to the vestibule floor, then shaking his raincoat from his shoulders, the raincoat sliding to his elbows, then to his wrists, then to his fingers.

The hostess drunk already as it's late and as it's her place and as she spent the better part of the week setting up for this evening with help from her two friends, lugging bags of bottles and candles into the house and painting walls and pounding nails into the walls and cleaning sinks and shaking rugs, and hoping, it's clear to me, that no one will ruin the evening, as things are as they should be, crowded, candlelit, somewhat drunken, and knowing, as I do, that things often get ruined by other things, by an over-drunk guest, for instance, knocking into walls or slipping on a rug or climbing the staircase to an upstairs place to wake the neighbors who sit at home alone in the evenings, the neighbors who peer through their peepholes, rather than open their doors, and who call the cops, insisting that the music be shut down, that the crowd disperse, that the hostess sit alone on her bed for the rest of the evening as she does many evenings.

The last guest crossing the threshold, pushing through the crowd, pushing through the room where I sit by a window, pushing through the kitchen where the hostess sees him pass and straightens, then pushing into the bedroom of the hostess where he drops his wet raincoat to the pile of wet coats piled high on the bed.

The hostess hoping, mostly, it seems, that this redhead will show, made obvious in her sudden though sloppy alertness when he crosses the threshold late and she attempts to straighten her sloppy stance, then attempts to follow him through the crowd in her tight backless dress, wobbling on pencil-thin heels, and made up, I don't have to say like what, just heavily, though fading, running, will suffice, and pushing, too, through the crowd as if on a mission, pushing everyone out of her way, saying, Has anyone seen my cat, looking to the floor as if for the cat, then up to the face of the last guest to arrive whom she stops, pressing her palm flat to his chest, on his way from the bedroom where he has left his raincoat on the top of the coat heap, Have you seen my cat, No.

Arriving early and knocking on the door, and the hostess saying, Help yourself, to a drink, to a chair, and helping myself to the chair by the window in a room as no one else sits yet in that room and as the chair faces the door to the vestibule where one can watch guests arrive and push into the bedroom where they leave their wet coats on the bed.

Knowing none of the guests, not even knowing, really, the hostess, who rarely utters more than an occasional weak hello, eyes averted, in the vestibule or out on the grass.

His red hair, this last guest, from where I sit watching him talk to the hostess, who strikes a match for his cigarette and who clutches his elbow when a heel goes wobbly, this one's red hair reminding me of a boy from seventh grade, a new kid with hair the same shade of red, and the same translucent eyes and lashes, and uncanny the sameness in the shape of the face, this guest pushing through with those same thin hips, the same liquid swagger, first one jutting hipbone then the other, a sort of swivel, which reminds me, also, of another kid from seventh grade, a boy-looking girl I hang out with before the day I move with my mother to another place for a different school, for eighth grade that is, the detail to remember, the move for eighth, as I have been taken by my mother from the first school and its bad influence, this boy-looking girl who says of this redheaded kid at school, Firebush, whispering it into my ear in every class he's in with us, especially science as we sit behind him and see how the hair molds to his neck in small flame-shaped waves, and we are no good anyway with science, Firebush, when he walks past in the hallway holding his books loosely, walking in that liquid swagger, that cocky fuck-you walk I fall for, Firebush, her lips pressed to my ear.

Two cops shining flashlights in the window near the chair where I sit, and striking, with the flashlights' lightbeams, his red hair across the room, so that for a moment his hair glows as if on its own, as if the light shines from within his head or from within each thread of hair, looking like not just fire but something more, the sun, perhaps, or some kind of holy fire rather than some scientific fire, more like a painted golden halo of sorts and less like the fire burning in science off a curl of soft metal, and if you look it blinds you says the teacher, and so we look, and the hostess noticing, too, this golden halo and looking startled into his lighted hair before noticing the lightbeams, how the light just comes from flashlights shining from the other side of the window, and the hostess saying, Shit, the cops.

Smoking in this boy-looking girl from seventh grade's bedroom the thin, brown cigarettes her mother smokes and leaves in packs on the kitchen table for us to steal, not meaning for us to steal them, but not understanding how we cannot resist any temptation, including smoking, including starting fires in the basement, including calling this new kid on the telephone from this girl's dismal bedroom, this new kid whose mother is now the crossing guard at school and wears blue cop-pants and stands on the corner outside their house to help us cross the street, but we never cross at the corner knowing we are too old to need help crossing a street and would rather cross a block away and cut through her backyard garden and hide behind the neighbor's tree hoping we will see the new kid walk out from his house, but we never do, and calling him after school, whispering into the telephone through a thin sweater to muffle our voices, Can we come over, Can we touch your firebush.

Living above the hostess and often hearing her in her bedroom from my bedroom crying to her friends on the telephone in the evenings that no one likes her in the way she wishes one would like her.

The cops knocking hard on the door and asking the two friends of the hostess who answer the door if they can please get the hostess, the cops' stiff hats in their hands dripping rainwater onto the vestibule floor, and the hostess walking wobbly in her pencil-thin heels and tight backless dress, holding a dishtowel to use to dry the floor, which gets wetter the more the cops stand there dripping and dripping, and the hostess saying, Hiya fellas, and the cops saying, Turn down the music, We've had complaints.

Thinking of approaching him, this last guest, of saying, Okay, it's you and me now, or, Come with me, or, Let's split this scene, as there is something that needs to be said about how he resembles this kid, It's uncanny, What, You look just like this kid from seventh grade, So, And could easily be him, the older version of this kid who now, like me, of course, is older, and thinking of what could happen if he, the last guest, would just play with me a bit, If you would just humor me and pretend to be this kid from seventh grade, And why would I do that, So that I can work a few things through.

The two friends of the hostess locking themselves in the bedroom to fuck, and everyone knowing that this is why they have locked up in the bedroom, first, as they're drunk, the two friends, all evening stumbling about the place from room to room, and, second, as they've been groping each other all evening, as well, provoking more than one guest to utter the predictable, Get a motel room, provoking the friends to take the bedroom and not come out despite an occasional hard knock on the door, despite leaving the hostess stumbling about drunk on her own, despite the fact that other guests' coats are piled high and drying on the bed, a selfish move, perhaps, on the part of the two friends who are only, obviously, thinking of themselves and of fucking, but a favor, somewhat, to the hostess, as no one can get his or her coat when it's time to leave and it's raining, so that no one leaves unless willing to leave with no coat, so that everyone stays somewhat late.

Thinking of approaching this guest, now that he stands alone, now that the hostess is looking at the cops' wet black boots, now that the cops are stooped and drying the floor with their own handkerchiefs, it looks like, boys being boys, even the ones in blue too flirtatious to let her use her clean dishcloth on the wet and muddied vestibule floor, one cop flirtatious enough to pick up the pressed out cigarette of the last guest and present it to the hostess as if it were a rose, and the hostess unsure of what to do, unsure, one can tell, if this is a flirtatious move on the part of the cop and so she accepts the crushed cigarette with two fingers, and the last guest not watching this, not watching the hostess, but lighting a cigarette and standing by a wall, alone, watching what seems to be nothing but is really the window, behind which seems to be nothing.

Calling the new kid on the telephone and the new kid saying, Leave me alone, and us saying, Let me touch you, and him saying, Who is this, and us saying, It's your mother, and him saying, I'll kill you girls, and us saying, Fuck you then, and him saying, Fuck you then, and us saying, Okay, fuck us.

Holding the door to the vestibule open for the hostess in the daytime as she lugs her bags of paper plates and paper napkins and bottles and candles up the sidewalk and to the door and says to me with no perceptible emotion, Come tonight if you like, and both of us knowing I am invited as what seems a courtesy but is really a selfish move on the part of the hostess, knowing that one must invite all of one's neighbors, dull or not, who live in the house or in surrounding houses to lessen the risk of calls to the cops from one's always-home neighbors always complaining of noise.

The hostess unaware of how thin her ceiling is, unaware of how much can be heard though my floor, her ceiling, like her crying in the evenings on the telephone to friends, crying, I hate my life, before she decides an evening with friends will fix things.

The hostess squeezing back through the crowd, still clutching her dishcloth, saying, Turn it down, to whomever can turn it down, and, when it's turned down so that those close enough can make out the sounds of the friends in the bedroom, and I don't have to go into the details of these sounds, the sounds of the bedsprings and so on, and when the cops seem to have left for good after one last, Don't make us come back, said in a possibly flirtatious way as if daring the hostess to make them come back, the hostess saying, Turn it back up, and, when the music is up and loud enough to feel it in one's bones, the hostess dancing for us, for the crowd, pulling her dress over her knees so that one can see she wears nothing under her dress, and all the guests watching, clapping, as she shakes herself out, fanning herself with the dishcloth, everyone laughing, except for the last guest who stands against a wall watching what seems to be nothing but is really the window where two headlights shine inside and light his hair, and the hostess seeing the light on his hair as she has been looking at him and hoping, it seems, that he will look back, but he never does, and the hostess looking outside and pulling down her dress, though not all the way, and

saying, Turn it down, to whomever can, and opening the door to
the vestibule where the cops stand dripping rainwater to the floor,
Hiya fellas, Turn down the music, I did already, We've had complaints, Well, who's complaining, Look miss, Are you complaining,
We'll arrest you miss.

Knowing that to show one must pretend to like the hostess and her
preparations for evenings such as these, her incessant pounding of
nails which gives one a headache and the incessant paint fumes
which drift though the cracks in the ceiling and rise through one's
floor and worsen the headache, not to mention the awful dust
floating up when she shakes her rugs, the dust floating through
one's window which makes one want to march downstairs to the
hostess and say, Stop that fucking shaking already, Stop that fucking pounding.

Knowing that to show one must pretend to have never been bothered by the sounds of drunken guests from prior evenings at the
home of the hostess fucking in the bedroom below one's bedroom,
therefore, provoking one to get oneself off, yes, imagining a three-
some with the drunken friends, as other over-drunk guests stumble
up the staircase to pound on doors in the most drunken minutes of
their evening, interrupting, calling, Wake up everyone, before the
hostess lures them back downstairs with a flash of her legs, as seen
through the peephole.

Knowing that to be there when cops arrive, for cops will always
arrive despite who has been invited, is to say to the hostess, I am
not the neighbor who complains, I can be trusted, I deserve the
invitation.

Calling this new kid until he leaves his telephone off the hook and all we get is the busy signal, and we are stuck, the two of us, sitting in her dismal bedroom on the dusty shag rug, looking at each other and bored with nothing to do but science now that we have smoked all the cigarettes.

Thinking of saying to the last guest, Come with me, to pull him somewhere, though not to my place as his knowing where I live is his knowing I am a neighbor and that I was invited only as a selfish move on the part of the hostess, his knowing quite well, as do all the guests, as do I, that her neighbors are of the pathetic and dull sort, the always-home sort, everyone knowing, too, that to invite one's neighbors is to reduce the risk of calls to the cops, and thinking of getting the last guest, therefore, into the bedroom of the hostess, after, and if, the two friends come out, and doing something in there with him, something risky, something involving some kind of role-play in which his role is that of the new kid from seventh grade who, when I go to return my tray in the cafeteria, grabs my tits from behind and squeezes hard, pressing his cock against my ass, saying, Stop calling me, and, You're ugly, leaving me crying and curled on the cafeteria floor with a crowd of kids around my body.

A fire starting and spreading in the kitchen sink from candles lighted around the sink as a decorative move on the part of the hostess and her two friends who helped to decorate all week for this evening, and too many drunken guests throwing their paper plates and napkins to the sink to catch fire, and the flames seeming quite capable of growing, of reaching a good height, a height that could scorch the cabinets above the sink or the ceiling above the cabinets, that is, my floor, the ceiling.

Often hearing the hostess in the evening crying to herself, a poor pathetic crying, a please-feel-sorry for-me sort of sobbing that lasts, often enough, until something is broken against a wall or against the ceiling above which I stand.

The hostess walking back to where the last guest is, before I can approach him, before I can even rise from my chair, the hostess taking hold of his elbow, not seeing the fire growing in the kitchen sink, and saying, Have you seen my cat, and him saying, No, and her saying, Let's go outside, trying her hardest to lure this last guest into the rain for a walk through the wet grass as the bedroom is occupied, still, by her two fucking friends, Barefoot, No thanks, Why not, I don't know, Come on, No.

Setting our science on fire in the boy-looking girl's basement, as neither of us understand science and neither of us care to understand anything quite so confusing as science with all its plants and metals and space and sex, and watching as the pages burn one by one, blackening in her mother's glass ashtray.

Often hearing the hostess in her bedroom from my bedroom calming herself down, singing softly to herself, the faint squeak of the bedsprings as she sits.

Both of us too slow to stop a single curl of burning science which has released itself from the corner of a page and floats slow-motion in the air like something holy or something cosmic, scientific, a comet, or a meteor, whichever one burns, if either, and watching it land to burn a strip of scorch in the basement shag before we stomp it out and run to my house unsure of whether we stomped it out completely.

Often hearing the hostess in her bedroom from my bedroom getting herself off in some way, knowing, always, she is alone doing this, getting herself off, as there is only one voice, always, if any, her voice, faint, and the sound I know is the bed, the faint creaking of bedsprings, and wanting, always, for her to stop.

Days after school so dull and nothing after this kid stops answering the telephone, after smoking all the brown cigarettes and destroying all our science with fire and running to my house hoping the fire is out at hers and hoping not to hear sirens on their way to her burning-down-house where her mother will not be until night, and playing in my bedroom a game we call CB radio that goes, Breaker breaker, what's your handle, over, Breaker breaker, what's yours, over, My handle's Kitten, what's your handle, over, Man of Steel here, Kitten, over, Where are you, Man, over, I'm next to you in the blue truck, over, Well, you're cute, Man of Steel, over, Well, so are you, Kitten, over, Well, let's pull over and do it, over.

Fire spreading from the kitchen sink to the counter, and the hostess seeing the fire and running to the sink and trying to put out the fire on the counter with her dishtowel, and the dishtowel catching fire, and the hostess waving it frantically, drunkenly, screaming, Help me, before she slams it to the floor and stomps it with her heels, not able to put out the fire with those wobbly pencil heels, and everyone surrounding, laughing at her, except the last guest who walks slowly over to where she is, who lifts the burning dishcloth from the floor and, holding it an arm's length from his body, slowly lowers it into the sink and turns the faucet to extinguish the fire before pressing the now wet dishcloth to the fire spreading along the counter.

Flashing our bodies, one part at a time, me as Kitten and her as Man of Steel, often forgetting who is who, then a dry and lipless makeout, feeling each other up under the bed, eyes squeezed shut.

Singing to myself in my room so as not to hear the hostess below me, so as not to have her hear me pressing my ear to the floor, but, rather, so that she hears me singing to myself, minding my own business singing, poorly, faintly.

The hostess clapping, saying, Yes, as all the fire turns to smoke, and the last guest with fire rising from his hand and no one moving to help him as he walks from the kitchen, holding his burning hand close to his face.

The boy-looking girl showing me a note from the new kid that says, Meet me in the woods Friday, saying she is going to the woods by his house to show him her tits and that they will kiss with tongues and more and to tell her mother, if she doesn't get back until late on Friday and if her mother calls my house looking for her, that she is staying at school late for a club or some such, What club, Make one up.

Running to the last guest, whose hand is on fire, from my place in the chair by the window and pulling him, by his thin wrist, back to the kitchen and plunging his hand to under the still-running faucet to put out the fire, and the hostess watching, clearly annoyed.

The boy-looking girl sitting on her kitchen counter, mixing water and sugar in a paper cup and telling me to taste it, saying this is what it will taste like when she does what she does in the woods with the new kid on Friday, and tasting it and finding it tastes very confusing, not at all like sugar, not at all like water.

The hostess giving a look as if to say, How dare you touch my guest, and the last guest giving an equally annoyed look as if wondering who I am, where I have come from, why I am plunging his thin hand into the cluttered sink of hardened wax and scorch in front of the other guests, none of whom I know, when he was clearly not on fire, clearly fine, both of us walking away from the sink, me following him, I'm sorry, It's okay, I thought you were on fire, I wasn't, I'm sorry, It's okay.

Me and the boy-looking girl in the woods after school, her taking me to where she will meet the new kid on Friday, her starting a small campfire in a circle of rocks with twigs and balled up notebook paper and a box of matches, her showing me what she will do with the new kid, how she will lift up her shirt like this, how she will unbutton his pants like this, saying, Breaker breaker, into her fist, then flattening our bodies to the grass like cats, and rolling in the grass, our eyes squeezed shut, before stomping out the fire in the circle of rocks, before buttoning our pants, before walking home, her saying she will kick my legs black and blue if I ever tell anyone anything.

The crossing guard's backyard garden where we once go for science to taste new lettuce and new carrots just pulled from the dirt and which still have dirt on them when we eat them and taste, to me, like mud, and everyone else, the teacher, the students, the crossing guard, proclaiming they are so sweet, the tiny carrots, the wrinkled lettuce leaves, just pulled from the garden, and the confusion when something is supposed to be sweet and I am supposed to know what sweet means, what it tastes like, but the something sweet does not taste sweet to me at all, but bad, like mud, like sugarwater, like the new kid is supposed to taste, and seeing this girl chewing on her carrot, and seeing the new kid chewing, and running into the house feeling sick, feeling like I am going to throw up, and throwing up on my shirt, on the crossing guard's waxed kitchen floor, the new kid coming in and seeing and calling for his mother who calls my mother.

Standing near the bedroom door behind the last guest, waiting for the friends to come out, both of us waiting to get into the bedroom, him knocking on the door to get in there sooner, and me knocking on the door from behind him.

The new kid's mother giving me a clean shirt to wear, giving me a place to sit in the quiet house, a place to wait for my mother to show, waiting even after the kids from class have left, the new kid waiting outside under a tree, and I can see him through the window, not wanting to come back inside until I leave.

The friends, at last, coming out from the bedroom, looking worn, unbuttoned, giving the last guest dirty looks for knocking, for interrupting, as I quickly push him into the bedroom and enter the bedroom behind him and shut the door, despite his struggling, despite his confusion, and lock the door, and the other guests pounding on the door from the other side, insisting we let them in to get their coats, screaming, Let us fucking in, and the last guest trying to unlock the door but my hand is over the lock, and the last guest saying, Let them in, and, before I can explain, the last guest, standing behind me, succeeding in pulling my hand away from the door, quite roughly, and unlocking the door and allowing the guests to rush into the bedroom to peel their coats from the heap, so that they can leave in the rain.

In the cafeteria, the boy-looking girl watching me walk to return my tray, watching as the new kid grabs my tits, roughly, from behind and presses his cock against my ass, and yes in seventh grade, and yes his cock, though in seventh grade we call it a dick, and I don't have to say what it feels like, seventh grade or not, and I don't have to say again how he calls me ugly, how his dick is pressing hard enough to make me crumble, and this boy-looking girl running over as if to get me up off the floor after I crumble, as if to save me, but kicking me, instead, in the legs and trying to kick his legs, as well, before he walks away laughing, pushing through the crowd and disappearing.

Standing in the bedroom and the two friends walking back in to retrieve their coats which have been on the bottom of the coat heap all evening as they were the first to arrive, and the two friends finding, beneath their coats, the cat, small, curled beneath the coats, and finding, too, that their fucking on the already heavy weight of the drying coat heap has hurt the cat.

The boy-looking girl's mother calling my house on Friday evening, and my mother saying, No she's not, and, Yes she's home, and, Yes you can, and handing me the telephone with a look on her face as if to ask if I am in trouble, and taking the telephone and telling her mother, when she asks where the hell her girl is, that she's at school for a club I think, Which club, I don't know which, Well, what did she say, Nothing, Well, you said a club, A music club, She doesn't do music, Science then, Put your mother on the phone.

The hostess getting herself off in her bedroom in the evenings, and hearing from my bedroom the faint sounds of her and pressing my ear hard to my floor, singing softly all the while, yet pressing to my floor, her ceiling, to better hear her.

Realizing the crossing guard has given me one of the new kid's shirts, that there are no instructions on washing it and returning it, that she has most likely forgotten that she even lent out the shirt, and my mother trying to wash it to return it before I rescue it from the pile of laundry on the laundry room floor and hide it in my pillowcase, taking it out at night, reading the letters on the front of the shirt which spell something, the name of a school, not ours.

Hearing sirens from my house when cops go past in search of this boy-looking girl, and the cops, later, coming to my house and telling me and my mother that they have searched the girl's house where her mother is frantic, that they have searched the school-yard, the classrooms, finding nothing, no one, except those who are truly in clubs for things like music and science and have not seen her, ever, and the cops questioning me about this girl's where-abouts, saying, Come on miss, trying to make me spill how this girl is going to kiss the new kid with her tongue and do other things in the woods, saying, Where is she miss, I don't know.

The two friends calling it an accident, calling it uncanny how the cat is hurt, blaming the noise, the crowd, saying that the cat had to hide somewhere, blaming the hostess, deciding that the cat could not take the crowd, the noise, and hid, and how uncanny as cats are not easily crushed but slide out from under piles with ease, say-ing that the hostess should have put the cat in a neighbor's place to sit with one of those pathetic always-home neighbors always doing nothing in the evenings, deciding that the hostess is to blame for the cat, that she is irresponsible as she hates her own life and cannot possibly care for the life of another, not even a cat, and the friends deciding to leave the cat where it is, suffering under their coats, until they know what to tell the hostess.

The cops telling my mother that they even have gone to the new kid's house to question his mother on whether or not the girl has crossed the street at the corner that day, not that we ever cross at the corner, and the cops telling my mother of a neighbor of the new kid noticing the cop car in front of the new kid's house and this neighbor coming outside of her own house to say, They're out of town, of the new kid and his mother, and me saying, That fucking liar, of the boy-looking girl, and my mother saying, What did you say, and me saying, Nothing, and the cops saying, Come on miss, and, as the girl, it turns out, is a liar, and is, therefore, nothing but talk, me telling the cops that perhaps the girl is in the woods, alone, that she often goes to the woods by the crossing guard's house to be alone, and the cops leaving and finding her there in the woods sitting under a tree by a fire, and the girl calling me from her bedroom late Friday, after being driven home in a cop car, after being yelled at by her mother, and whispering to me, You're dead.

Everyone leaving, except me, except the last guest, as the hostess is clinging to him, begging him not to leave just yet, and except the two friends who are somewhat frantic in the bedroom, the hostess gripping the elbow of the last guest with one hand and fanning smoke with the scorched dishcloth with the other, saying good-night to the guests when they leave, fanning all the while toward the window where I, again, sit in a chair and breathe that smell of campfire in a circle of rocks, that smoke that stays on one's clothes for days, that scorched smell we can smell in each other's hair when we play CB radio, both of us Kitten and both Man of Steel, groping each other under the bed, and the hostess letting go of the last guest's elbow and sliding down the wall to kneel to pick up a crushed cigarette and staying there, slumped, looking as if she has forgotten something, like who she is, or where she is, the sky starting to lighten, despite the rain, the hostess slumped against the wall, looking faint by the last guest's feet.

In the cafeteria on Monday, sitting alone before the boy-looking girl comes over saying, You're dead, and me saying, You're a liar, and her saying, Fuck you, and me saying, Liar, and her saying, I'll kick you, and me saying, Fuck you, and her saying, I'll kick you I swear, before I get up to return my tray, before he, coming from somewhere, from I don't know where, grabs me from behind, saying, Ugly, in my ear, and, Stop calling me, before I crumble, before she kicks my legs and he walks off and my mother has to come get me.

The hostess fainting on the floor, her back against the wall, her legs out crooked like dolls' legs, her head crooked, too, hanging, mouth open, the last guest standing by her legs, unmoving, knowing he has decisions to make, at this point, as she faints, to wake her or not, to leave her or not, to fuck her or not, trying to see, one can tell, his near future, the late morning, the feeling of that.

The two friends trying to wake the hostess with a light tap on the arm, saying, Wake up, Wake up.

My mother laughing, saying, Boys will be boys, when she gets me at school the day I cannot pull my body off the dirty cafeteria floor after the new kid grabs my tits and calls me ugly and the girl kicks my legs and calls me lesbo and the crowd of kids is screaming, Lesbo lesbo, and the science teacher walking through and all the kids walking away and the science teacher leaning over me, saying, What is it, and, Can you get up, and then, when I do not get up, the science teacher calling down the hall to the school nurse, and the school nurse lifting me up from the floor as one would lift a heavy box and dragging me to her office and calling my mother and saying, Can you come up to school, saying, A boy teased her, then laughing at whatever it is my mother says and looking at me and laughing again, and my mother coming to get me from school, shaking her head, laughing, saying, Boys will be boys, trying to make me laugh on our walk past his house, past his mother stooped in her backyard garden, past the woods where I have rolled on the ground collecting dirt on my skin and hair, and my mother making faces to try to make me laugh, saying, Those dumb boys, and, I bet he likes you, and, I bet he's in love, patting me on the back, saying, Of course he's in love.

The two friends trying to wake the hostess who is not waking despite their occasional tapping, despite a harder prodding, despite the swift kick I deliver to her knee as a way to help her friends, and the hostess waking from my second kick and looking at me, furious, her hair a mess in her face, the hostess about to rise and destroy me she is so furious that I, the most unwanted guest, have kicked her in the knee, but saying, when she sees her friends, What, and the friends saying, The cat, and the hostess sobering up despite what she has had to drink and screaming, I don't have to say like what, suffice it to say loudly.

Rising from my bedroom floor, feeling perverted, uninvited, as if I have somehow fucked the hostess without her wanting to be fucked by me.

Telling my mother on our walk home that this girl makes me play this game, What game, that she makes me suck in my lips and kiss, that she makes me feel up her tits, That lesbo, What do you mean, Or she will kick my legs black and blue, my mother looking like she is going to yell or cry and covering her mouth and saying, What else does she make you do, Nothing, and me saying, Don't tell her mother, and her saying, You are not to play with her again, and me saying, Don't tell anyone anything, and my mother calling her mother when we get home and telling her mother that her daughter is a sicko lesbo, and me never telling my mother how it's often me who initiates CB radio, bored out of my head, saying, Breaker breaker, into my fist, saying, What's your handle, over, always thinking of getting off, never telling my mother how the girl has girl tits but a face like a boy, how it feels like something dirty when I'm with her, how I squeeze shut my eyes and think of the new kid and make her touch me harder down there until she gets bored which she always does and so I never get off, never telling how good it feels, later, in my bedroom, alone, rocking against a pillow or a stuffed animal or the pile of dirty laundry on my bedroom floor with flashes of being felt up by her or of being felt up by the new kid or of the new kid feeling her up in the woods with me watching and getting off watching or of her feeling him, even with her mouth, even with his sugarwater spurting out the campfire, all of it the same, a many-headed faceless groping sucking thing serving just one purpose, nothing holy, nothing with love, all of it science, some odd protrusion against some odd protrusion, then a burst of sparks, then a hollowness after the sparks go out, sitting blind, a girl again, waiting alone for dinner.

Calling the cops, despite the friends' attempts to disconnect the telephone, despite their screaming, Who are you even, as I say into the telephone to whoever answers when I call the cops, A cat was hurt, giving my address, despite the friends' attempts to get the telephone from my hand, despite the names they call me after I hang up, and I don't have to say what they scream or how they surround, the last guest not watching us but watching out the window for the cops.

Not having to finish school that year before my mother moves me somewhere else, and walking around in the daytimes like I am old or like I am some kind of ghost or something, translucent, walking past houses, walking past his house and past his house and past his house wearing his shirt, hoping the crossing guard does not see the edges of me walking around if she is digging in her garden or if she is standing on the corner in her blue cop-pants and hat, hoping I get to see him coming home from school, wanting to see him walking by himself down the street in that graceful fuck-you walk I fall for, the loose way he holds his books as if he wants to drop them, as if he wants to leave them there on the sidewalk and come with me into the woods.

The cops standing at the door, saying, Come with us, and the hostess and the two friends following the cops outside, one of the friends holding the cat, wrapped like an infant in her coat.

Watching from the chair the last guest walk from room to room, picking up bottles and dropping them into paper bags.

Deciding whether or not to come out of hiding, before he sees me standing there only half-hiding behind the tree in the neighbor's front yard like some kind of pervert, like some kind of sicko pervert wearing his shirt before he stops on the sidewalk so he does not have to pass me, so he does not have to face whatever sick thing it is I want, before he turns and runs back to school.

Watching the last guest put on his coat and open the door.

Knowing I should say, Stop.

Knowing he is scared of me, knowing he is scared of what I am thinking of doing with him because it's scary, I know, to be watched, but it's scarier, even, to be caught watching, and I cannot avert my eyes.

Wanting to say, Okay, it's you and me now, or, Let's split this scene, looking at the way his hair molds to his neck in those small flame-shaped waves, and wanting to say, Come with me now, but saying, instead, as he pulls the door to fully open, Who are you, and him saying to me with no perceptible emotion, except, perhaps, annoyance, and not even looking at me as he says it and not even wanting an answer, I can tell, Who are you, with the stress on the word *you*, as in Who the fuck are *you* annoying me, watching me, following me from room to room, though I didn't mean to annoy him, and meant, if anything, to work things through, and I still have the shirt.

Wanting to say, as if to explain, Look, and wanting to answer his question of who I am, to tell him who I am, to say something holy, something that will blow his fucking mind, as in, I am the one you ruined, as in, I am the one who ruined you, but saying nothing as he crosses the threshold and crosses the vestibule and disappears somewhere in the rain.

Invitation

Doors locked, he says, and windows up, radio off to be safe, *but why*, just off, he says, and, wear my jacket, *but why*, just wear it, your dress is too thin, *my dress is fine*, your dress, *it's fine*. But he warns, it's rough where I'm from, this place, *a dumb city*, you'll be looked at, gawked at, like mother like girl, the spitting image, *don't treat me dumb*. He says, it's not like home where I'm from, they're rough all these ones. And he knows these ones and these streets around here, that market, that church, that lighted tavern he knows like the back of his hand. He says, that's where we played, me and my pals, and that's where we parked, the things we did, you should ask your mother, *so what your pals*, we were crazy. The sun slips behind the rows of buildings, and the buildings are rundown, all

boarded up, and who isn't hungry, it's night already. He says, here's
a tavern, *but it doesn't seem decent*, so you're hungry right, so he says
and, so it's open. More than he can say for the rows of boarded
storefronts. This place is open. And this is real hunger. There was
nothing worth eating at that rundown wedding. Well, what do you
call this, he had held up his cake, *I call it nothing*, and he said, be
good, for once in your life. But that nothing cake, the bride's makeshift dress, *like sewn rags or some such*, and faded flowers, *carnations or
some such*, and he said, be good. But that rundown hall, her made
up face, *like a clown or something*, said for a laugh, and soon he said,
let's leave. And goodness he spun out to your chasing him, *are you
mad*, to nothing, *are you mad or something*, to his clenched teeth,
clenched hands, and good thing for the open car window, the
buildings whistling past, good thing for the radio on and up, *I know
this song*, and he snaps it off. Dumb, he says, like a headache or
something, and, I can't take you anywhere, and, roll up that window, and, that's where we killed time me and my pals, and that's
where we killed time. Though the rows of buildings are all boarded
up, all but this tavern, *I'm not going in*, and he says, fine, but it's an
unsafe street and he knows this street like he knows the back of his
hand. Not your home, he says, in my neck of the world, your
mother could tell you, ask your mother, knowing your mother
would strike him if she knew how quick he'd park you, leave you,
there on the street in a running car. Though he wants you to cover,
to wear his jacket. It all shows through that thin dress, he says. And
at least he's willing to stop. We'll eat here, he says, *I'm not eating inside*, and he says, fine, *I'd rather eat in the car*, and he says, fine then,
I'd rather use my fingers like a damn animal, and he says, animals don't
have fingers, and some such about the rough ones, *what ones*, those,
he says and slams the door, *hurry up*. And they stand by the church,
those ones, and they laugh standing there, poking each other with
sticks there laughing, spitting, and quick he's gone in the light of

the tavern. In the car is dark. And big deal they laugh, big deal
they walk with their heads jerking this way that way, and one says,
I'm not a, something or other, and what does it matter what he
says. The others say something loud, unclear, I'm not no, some
such or other, then a howl, a laugh, as they near the car. And remember rule one as they near. A look in the eyes is an invitation.
Everyone knows, even your mother. And then what. Trouble. The
worst kind. As in a stick to the skin, a strike, or worse. They go for
the ass, these ones, the tits, the face, even your father knows or he
wouldn't have said, wear my jacket. And so it's his fault all this
trouble, and it's his fault all this killing time, and it's his fault that
rundown wedding not worth the drive to the city. He's my best pal,
he said, *big deal*, my good old pal, he said, from when I was your
age, *big deal, I've got plans.* You're with me this weekend and you're
coming with me, *go yourself*, and he gave a, suit yourself, and the
crying, goodness, once it started it was hard to stop. He agreed so
quick, it seemed too quick and that he didn't care, his suit yourself,
and to send him alone meant his pal would have thought, your
girl's a something, your girl's no good, staying home for a boy. But,
stay at home, he said, it's too rough anyway, *I'll wear my new dress*,
it's too rough for you. Then a wait in the yard for his car. Your
mother in her nightgown waving from the window, be good!, as the
car lurched forward. Then a drive to the city and no one thought
to eat. They'll serve something at the wedding, so he said, they always do, but it was rundown cakes in a rundown hall, and who
doesn't want a decent wedding with none of this boarded up city,
these rundown streets. Who doesn't want a backyard wedding under trees and stars, a springtime wedding in the damn yard done
right, father on one side mother on the other, a look deep into the
boy's eyes, and everyone knows it's for life, for love. Enough. This
is hunger. This is hunger playing with the head. This is a day of not
eating all day, and this is what happens after a day of not eating,

and soon he'll be back with something to eat. And soon he'll drive you away from this boarded up city. He'll drive you fast from these ones in t-shirts who poke each other with sticks. And they walk with their sticks, yelling, I'm not no, *what*, then a howl, then maybe a look. If they wanted they could. They could look at you. Then you could look back. Then they could break a window and reach with a hand. They could strike with their sticks, or worse. They could go for the skin, they could paw your tits, they could backhand you. And would he come from the tavern, would he yell, get off of her! But they're not looking. But they could look. They could take the car. And would he cry coming out to find no car or to find a shell of a car and nothing inside not even his jacket with the faded flower still pinned on. But this is just hunger talking, and no one's taking the car, and no one's going to strike you, and what flowers aren't lovely, even carnations are, even rundown brides, even in a dumb clown face and makeshift dress, admit it. And they danced right. Who didn't see the way they danced, the way his pal looked her deep, his hands clamped to her hips the whole time, goodness, the way he looked her so deep, who didn't feel it. And they played their song, that one, goodness, that one, whatever it's called, and he spun her about, they sweated like animals, spinning and grinding close and tight. Who didn't want to dance, even in that rundown hall, *can I dance*, even around those rundown people, *are you mad or something*, to his cake, *are you mad*, to nothing. He wasn't talking. He was mad at something. And you could have told him a thing or two to get him truly mad. You could have told him a thing about home, a thing of the boy you fell for. You should have told him, *you should see me up there, you should see me, there are nights, times, when you think I'm asleep, there's dancing in a parking lot and cigarettes and drinking from bottles up in our safe home, in springtime, in the summer,* but he went for his jacket, walking right past their animal dance. You should have told him, *on a street like this, rundown, dumb,* no it's different at home, hidden in trees *and there are cars and others and all the songs on and up and sitting in cars and big deal someone's fingers going all up and under and the heat from summer or smoke or a tongue going around and around my tongue and teeth and the pressure of fingers on my hips and it's songs up loud and shirts slipping to the floor of the car and our heads spinning out and out and* don't look, goodness no, eyes closed, goodness, a look in the eyes is an invitation. Everyone knows don't look or it's trouble. And one of the boys says, I'm not a, *what*, and another says, you got that all right, I'm not no, *you're not no what*. And they circle their slow wide circle past the market, the church, the tavern, the car, and they're young it seems, they're just boys in their t-shirts like the boy you fell for, and the sticks are not sticks but metal poles they sound as they scrape the cement. And they clang outside the church, and they clang outside the tavern, and he's inside the tavern and must have heard, or is the radio playing loud in there, and his songs or some such from his neck of the world, and is he dancing in there saying, my wife was no good, my girl's no good, like mother like girl, just dumb and dumb and dumb. But you're not dumb, you're not, or you would look at these boys as they move past the car, just a hip or a leg, now the bottom of a t-shirt brushing past. And don't look, not even a quick look, not even a safe look like the look at his old pal today dancing clamped to his bride, how your look could have turned harder and inward, a gawk, how it could have gone inside his head. He had eyes like the boy you fell for, the same dog eyes. They could have been brothers or father son. But he looked only at her, his dumb cheap bride, deep through, and who didn't feel it how it pinned her down, how anyone could see it this old pal looking deep through, pinning. And she let him pin her, she let that crazy song go on and on until she turned weak-kneed, *can I dance*, and he went for his jacket, and you danced your own circling dance alone to a time you should have told him, *a time with the boy when our tongues went and went and it tasted of cigarettes his spit how else could it have tasted and his hands were pressing and every part pressed up and hard and later his jacket spread under my legs and ass and our heads slipped to the floor of the car.* And you circled the chair until he came back with his jacket, he grabbed your arm and spun you out. *Are you mad at me,* to nothing but the car door slamming you in, the song going on and on, the wind messing your hair, thoughts of, there's a boy I fell for, and it could be love, the one true love, weak-kneed like the pal and bride, and he said, just like your mother, *what,* just like your mother, through clenched teeth, just like her, admit it, *what of it,* your mother. But she's clean. You're clean. Last time this boy you fell for said, look at me, you said no, knew a look was trouble, and you kept your eyes closed tight even with fingers up inside and the tongues pushing and every part pressing up and up. He said, what do you want, but rule two was don't answer, rule two was keep quiet even though it felt good, even though it felt crazy and could have been love. He said, tell me, *no,* before he started, tell me, *no,* and he was laughing, hands all over, pawing, saying, what do you want, saying, baby, you were crying, baby, and, look at these little things anyway, these little tits, and, I don't need these little tits, and you ran off, half-dressed, homeward to your father's house to cry in his backyard until morning. And he must have heard from the house, your father, your crying. And he did say the next day, how are you doing, or, are you well. But rule two was keep your words to yourself, even as he tried to make you talk, even as these boys try to make you talk, try to make you look with their words, their, I'm not no, *you're not no what.* But don't fall for it. It would be smarter not to. And the smartest thing would be to drive. It would be good and smart to drive from these boys, to spin the wheels out and up the street and wait. So what he'd walk out the tavern and he'd look all over, and so what you'd be at the end of the street, big deal. You'd never leave him. He knows this. It's something with blood. You'd be right there at the end of the street waiting, he knows. You'd push an arm through an open window, *over here dad!, hurry dad!* It would be good and smart to drive. But this is just hunger. And you're really fine now. You're better now. You're in your own safe place in the city, doors locked, windows up, and there's really no need to drive. The boys walk in a very wide circle. They walk past the market, the church, the tavern, the car. Besides, they look dumb as the boy you fell for. Besides, soon, he said or some such. Besides, who wants to drive. Besides, he'd walk out, he'd panic, he'd think, shit, the car, then, where'd she take it damn it, and besides, you haven't looked deep at these boys. You haven't invited a thing. You're safe. And besides, he'd walk out, he'd look all over saying, shit, the car, panicking. And they're not looking in yet. But they could look in. *But they're not.* But they could. They could hear the radio if you turned on the radio. *But it's off.* If you opened the window just a slit for air. *It's rolled up tight.* If you turned up the radio with the window a slit, they could hear, *big deal,* and they could get you, *and then what,* trouble. So drive up the street. You'd never leave him. You'd never think it, some such about blood. Just the boys could get rough. They could push a fist through the window or the poles or some such. They could try to paw you, to backhand you. But you could drive up the street. You'd yell, *up here dad!,* and he'd see the car. He'd think, what are you thinking, and you'd yell, *up here dad!,* and he'd see the boys, and he'd try and save you, he'd run to the car, and the boys' heads would jerk up, and they'd run to the car clanging their poles to the ground and again and again, *run faster dad,* you can see them running, *run faster dad,* and he says, coming to get you, but the boys are younger and running like dogs, spitting, get you get you, and the boys are the fastest, clanging their poles down and down and again and again and the boys yell, get you, *big deal,* gonna get you, and your father says, stay put, I'm coming to get you, and you thrust yourself to the hips out the window and look them all deep in their crazy dog eyes, just like a bride, and say, *hurry.*

To Sit, Unmoving

A man grabbed my father by his shirt. Then he punched my father's face.

My father fell backward into the street.

The man stooped in the street to my father. He pushed his fingers into my father's pants pocket. He fished out my father's wallet. Then he ran.

This was on the island. Puerto Rico. In the city. San Juan. On a street in the city. I don't know which. But the street was a low-lit street. And nothing was open on the low-lit streets that late at night but bars.

My father couldn't tell much of the man. There was a ski cap he said. A dark coat he said.

The fist before it reached his face.

What else, I said.

I mean I would have said.

I mean you would have said had you been sitting at the table in my father's office the following morning.

What I mean is had he been your father.

But there was nothing else.

My father fell backward into the street, his hands moving up to his eyes.

In the city were wild kids shooting up. Hookers poking from doorways.

This we heard from the man with the mustache who stood at the desk in the lobby.

The concierge, said my father to me and my brother, and he said it slow like, con-ci-erge.

The hotel limo wouldn't take us to the city. It would only take us to my father's factory and to other hotels that looked like ours. But my father said that this was stupid, that we were from a city and big deal this one he said.

I'll rent a sports car, he said. A red one, he said winking at my brother who lay on his side on the lobby floor.

In the city were wild dogs. Low-lit streets.

The concierge pulled his mustache in a way that looked like it should have hurt. But his mustache looked fake and I knew my brother would piss his pants if I said this.

You'll get stabbed in the city, the concierge said looking at me. He pulled on his mustache, and to my brother I said, Look, and pulled on the skin above my lip so it looked like it hurt. My brother laughed and rolled onto his back.

My father said, Stabbings. Big deal.

Stabbings, he said. We've got stabbings at home.

We had shootings as well. My brother and I heard shots at night from the park.

People walked over my brother and my brother tried to grab their legs.

My father said, We're from Bal-ti-more, and made his hand like he was holding a knife, ready to stab.

The concierge said, There are private restaurants here. In the good parts, he said. Keep to the private beaches, he said.

There was a Chinese restaurant in the hotel lobby and the inside looked like China. The Mexican one looked like Mexico and the music in each was different.

The lobby stores sold watches and gold chains and suntan oil. They sold American papers and American drinks. We liked the American drinks. We were Americans, and in America, or the States as my father told me and my brother to say, we drank regular drinks. We did everything regular in the States. We weren't stuck in the States in a dull hotel. We could walk after school to the city park. We could walk home alone at night.

My father threw some dollars to the desk. He said, Sports car. Red. My brother thought this was funny. This, because my brother's brain was wired wrong. He wasn't retarded. But his brain told him to do things other ways. Like sometimes it told him to laugh a lot. Sometimes it said to be silent. There were days we could poke and poke him in the ribs and he still wouldn't say one word. Those days he wore his headphones. He listened to metal and my father said, You'll rot your brain.

My father nudged my brother with his foot. He said, Get up, son, and my brother grabbed my father's leg.

The concierge spoke Spanish on the phone. We knew he was talking shit about us. We were white, as if you didn't know this. We were stupid white fuckers. We were rich white fucks.

This is not anger. I am not angry.

We sat nights, my father on dates, in the hotel room. There was nowhere else to go. We could play on the sidewalk outside the hotel just until it got dark. Just until the concierge shooed us back inside. At nights the lobby stores were closed. And we were not allowed on the beach. Dangerous kids hung out on the beach after dark. The concierge said, Do you want to get killed, and my brother made a gun with his hand and said, Pow. Nights we ordered room service and charged it to the room. There was American food on all the menus. We ordered from the American side. But it all tasted weird and Puerto Rican. The hamburgers came on regular bread. The potatoes were bananas. The TV shows were all in Spanish. Only some words were English. Chevrolet. Golden Skillet. My brother laughed at the cartoon commercials. There was one for chicken, one for something else. A drink.

To say my father was an inventor would be to lie. He mostly invented things that didn't work. In fact, only one thing worked, and you couldn't call someone an inventor when he invented only one thing that worked.

It would be to say I was a killer because I had one murderous moment one night with some kids in the park.

It would be to say my brother was a genius because he had one good idea, just one, once, slamming into the soft walls of his rotted brain.

The things my father built that didn't work were kept in boxes in a room in our house in the States. I never knew what these things were supposed to do, but there were wires and powders and pieces of foam in boxes, always, in this room in the house.

When he invented the one thing that worked, at last, a filter of all things, a filter that clicked into some kind of mask that workers in factories would strap to their faces in order to breathe, he took me and my brother to California. A celebration. My mother was dying and couldn't go. I mean to say she was literally dying. My father said, You could use the air, but she said, Go, to my father and went back to sleep.

My father took us to a restaurant that overlooked a city. Los Angeles, I think, but we were so far up on the top of a hill it didn't matter what city it was.

My father called the waitress darling. He held her by her wrist. He ordered a bottle of wine. Three glasses, he said and winked at my brother. He talked about things we didn't understand. He said his filter could take dust from the air. It could crush the dust to smaller bits. The waitress laughed and said, I don't get it. She walked away.

People want to breathe, my father said. I'm an inventor, for the love of God.

My brother drank his wine like it was water, and my father said, Easy, son.

He smacked the table. Do you hear me, he said.

My brother looked up.

Not you, said my father. Your sister, he said. She never listens.

Below us the city's white lights blinked. It could have been home how it looked. It could have been me and my brother dusted in sand, high up in the city park.

My father said the waitress was a dog.

My brother looked about to laugh.

A toast, said my father.

We raised our glasses.

To dust, he said.

Dust was mostly human skin. I learned this in school.

My brother barked at the waitress.

My father touched our glasses with his glass.

When the man in the coat and cap ran off my father rose to his knees. He must have looked like he was praying. Or like he was drunk. Motionless, touching his bloody face. Struggling to stand while holding his nose. Then the blood between his fingers. Dirt on the knees of his pants.

No big deal, he said.

He could wash the pants.

And he had nothing in the wallet.

A couple bills, he said.

And the wallet was a cheap one bought on the island.

His license. No big deal.

You can replace a license, my father said. They give anyone a license on this backward island.

Even the ladies, said my father.

He was with a date in the city. She worked in my father's factory.

He said, She's the best looking one. Her hair. It's danger.

Hot to fucking trot, he said.

Before the date, he took me and my brother for a ride in the sports car around the hotels. The tires squealed. My brother screamed when the car went faster.

My father said, That's right, son. He said, This is the life.

He stopped the car outside the hotel. He said, This is your stop. He said, I've got a date. He said, Hot to trot. He slapped my brother on the back. Be good, he said.

We were in his office the following morning. My father had spent the night in the office. He had called us before he went to sleep. He said, I'm working late. Go to sleep, he said. But we watched TV instead.

In the morning the concierge knocked on the door. He said, Let's go. We would ride in the limo to my father's factory. The limo was better than the sports car. We could see out the windows of the limo, but no one could see us in it. People always tried to see inside. Kids pushing their bikes up the street. Ladies in cars beside us. When I gave them the finger my brother laughed.

There were plates of eggs and fruit on a table in my father's office, but we didn't eat. My father had two black eyes, a blood-crusted nose. His words sounded thick and slurred.

He said, I was barely out of the car and this guy, he grabbed me. He punched me. I fell backward to the street. And my nose was bleeding like hell.

He and the date were getting some drinks in the city.

I'm allowed, he said.

He said, Isn't that right, son. He looked at my brother who looked at the silver pitcher on the table. The pitcher curved inward then out. On the inward, things looked upside-down. My brother and I liked to look at ourselves in the pitcher. We looked wild and snake-haired and monstrous.

It wasn't a pitcher you put things in.

My father said, Don't touch the pitcher.

He said, Touch it and die.

He was looking at me.

Five hundred dollars, he said, it cost me.

Keep off it, he said.

I didn't touch it, I said.

You were about to, he said.

My brother couldn't look at my father's face. I had to look.

My father said, A knuckle sandwich. Pow, he said.

He nudged my brother and said, Pow.

My father said, She liked the car. Of course she liked the car, he said. They all like the car. She turned everything on. The radio. Click. The heater. Click. He said, Click click click, and looked at my brother to make him laugh. Click, he said and poked my brother in the gut.

My brother got up from the table and sat on the floor.

My father said, A son of a gun.

When the filters filled with dust they were trashed. Then the trash was poured into landfills. And landfills were full of rats. My father should have known this. He went to school. He should have known about landfills. And about rats. How these rats had very sharp teeth. How they could find the filters in the landfills. How they could chew straight through the filters.

You're crazy, said my father.

He said to my brother, Your sister's crazy.

My brother laughed.

But I knew dangerous dust was released by rats.

It became a part of the air again.

My brother wasn't retarded. He just couldn't learn right. His brain made things backward. Like his right and left. And telling time. And he couldn't tie shoes. He wore slip-on sneakers. The kind with the Velcro. They always looked crooked, too big for his feet.

It's a phase, said my father.

He's a genius, he said.

But my brother and I knew better. His brain was our secret. Only he and I knew how truly fucked up it was.

My father said, It's because of your mother.

She was sick, then dead.

But that wasn't it.

The masks were sewn in a factory on the island. The factory was small and made only masks. Bigger factories made the filters. These were in Baltimore and I had been to these factories with my brother. They were big and full of workers working big machines. The workers were men who smoked while they worked. No one talked. They didn't like me and my brother running around. We tried to push buttons on the machines when the men weren't looking, and my brother would squeal like a fucking retard and the men would say to my father, Get these kids out, and come walking at us in a slow monster way that made my brother squeal even harder, and I was the one to tell the workers to get back to work, and they laughed at me, like, Who the fuck does she think she is, but they knew who I was.

At some point they would be working for me.

We all liked the island factory better. The workers on the island were ladies who spoke Spanish and played with my brother's hair. My father went to the island over the summers. It used to be he went alone. But now he had to take us.

Weekends we stood in the ocean. We collected snails in a bucket and raced them on the sand. My father slept on a chair. We put snails on my father's feet to make him jump. He said, What the hell. He didn't shave on the weekends. The ladies around him laughed when he jumped.

There were crazy kids who climbed the palms. They picked coconuts and split them up with a knife. They sold them one for a dollar to me and my brother. They told us we were stupid fucks. They said, They're free if you climb the tree. Neither of us could climb a tree with no branches. They said we were rich white fucks. We already knew this. The boys didn't wear shoes or shirts. They're free, they said. But we gave them the dollars.

My father called the kids the Coco Locos.

He said, Keep away from those dirty kids.

We went weekdays to my father's office. It had a glass door. On the other side of the door was the factory. We could see the ladies hunched over their tables, sewing masks. The ladies couldn't see us in the office though. The door was like the limo windows. I liked to be on the unmirrored side. Though sometimes I couldn't help it. Sometimes there were limos with other people in them. And I was with my brother on the mirrored side. We were playing on the hotel sidewalk. And I wanted to look in the mirror. But I knew better than to look too hard. Even my brother knew someone could be giving the finger.

When the ladies used the mirror to fix their lipstick, my father stood on our side and said, Stupid estupidos. Sometimes he opened the door into the ladies. Sometimes he said something funny like, Working hard I see.

The ladies took breaks from sewing masks. There was pan de agua and coffee. They prayed before eating by closing their eyes and moving their lips.

They're devout, said my father. De-vout. Good ones, he said.

I had heard my father ask the ladies to dinners. Lucky you darling, my father would say. Good food darling. Buena comida.

I'm allowed, he would say to me and my brother.

I had seen my father touch the ladies. I had seen him touch their asses.

My father's coffee was the blackest made in his own pot. The ladies spooned him sugar.

Some ladies wore masks after eating their pan de agua. The factory air was dusty.

Once I said, Funny.

My father said, What.

Dust, I said. Here.

He said, You don't know funny.

In Baltimore was the park on the hill where under the sand was wet.

China, I said, if you dig deep enough.

My brother's sneakers never looked right.

There were days I could barely look at him.

In the park were monkey bars. Rusted swing sets.

There was a slide where we slid into sand.

My brother and I went to the park after school. The monkey bars at the park were higher than the ones in the schoolyard. We perched on the monkey bars and watched the sunset. The sky turned orange. Then back to blue. We could see the whole city lighted below. We never talked. We sometimes heard gunshots. We mostly listened to traffic.

There was a time my father would say to me, One day it's yours.

All of it, he would say.

He would gesture to what. A hotel room. A factory. A view. The leather inside of a rented car.

And I would say, I don't want it.

And he would say, You don't know what you want.

And I would say, I know what I don't want.

And he would say, You don't know shit.

And my brother would put his headphones on and turn up the metal and rock his head in a retard way.

And my father would look at me.

And the feeling in my gut.

When my father called England and France he waved us away and mouthed, England, or, France. He said, Go.

Outside goats ate the parking lot weeds. My brother and I threw sticks to the goats. They were so stupid these island goats. Sometimes they ate the sticks. And sometimes they came running at us like dogs.

The ladies' husbands pulled into the lot. They waited in their cars in cotton shirts. They smoked cigarettes down to the filters and flicked their filters to the lot. All of the goats would go after the filters. The husbands never laughed at the goats. Their windows were open even in rain. Fast-speed island music played. When the husbands waved we looked at the ground.

On the low-lit street, the date ran off.

Sure she ran, my father said. She was scared, he said. She's young.

He wore a ski cap, he said. Imagine. A coat.

On an island for God's sake, said my father.

He said, Who wears a coat on an island.

Then pow, said my father.
Sure she ran.
Brass knuckles, he said.
Lousy island, he said.
He pulled my nose.
Eat your eggs, he said.

Maryland. Shaped like a gun. The city not far from the trigger. A house in the city. A bedroom in the house. A bed in the bedroom pushed to the wall. Under the blanket. Morning in winter. A
streak of light piercing the curtain. Dust forming in the streak of
light. A single dot of dust. Its flight across the room.

On a ride in the sports car, it was me and my father's date
in the back.
The best looking one in the factory, he said. Boy look at that
body. Out to here.
Look at her body boy, said my father. You won't see that in
the States.
My brother sat in the front. He read a comic and listened
through headphones.
The spitting image, said my father slapping his back. A son
of a gun.
This was a Friday. He drove us to a dinner in the city. We
took the highway. We were speeding to get there. The lady drivers
were the worst said my father. The ladies shouldn't even have a
license, he said. Watch this, he said as he cut one off. Watch this.
They swore in Spanish at my father.

He said, That'll show them to mess with a genius.

A man in San Juan grabbed my father's shirt. He punched my father's face. My father fell.

So this was my father lying in the street. My father with a bloody nose. Blood on his best cotton shirt. My rich white American father, an inventor of something that let people breathe.

This wasn't your father.

I wish it had been yours.

Then I could say the right things to you and we could have a drink and maybe laugh at the thought of your father all fucked up in the street.

But your father would never have been lying on some low-lit street in San Juan.

Your father would never have been bleeding like that, like some stupid fucker, just bleeding like that.

I asked my father about the dust.

I said, Where does it go.

He said, It goes in the filter.

It gets crushed, he said.

Then what, I said.

He said, It stays in the filter.

But what if it gets out, I said.

He said, It won't get out.

I said, But what if rats in the landfills chew through the filters.

He said, Rats cannot chew through the filters.

I said, Yes they can.

He said, No they can't.
I said, Yes they can.
He said, Do you want to be poor.

There was a day my brother and I were looking through my father's failed inventions for no good reason other than my mother would die and she wanted the house clean, and we were cleaning the room where he kept his failed inventions, his assembled bits of wire and foam and string and metal, and we laughed pretty hard when my brother picked up some crazy looking object, an object that looked like a robot built by retard kids, and I remember saying, What the fuck, and my brother said, Look, and put the object on a table and pushed a small red button on its front, and the whole thing shook then split in two.

When my brother and I perched on the monkey bars no one could see us. It was too dark. And we were too high up. Not even the kids who stood below us could see us up there.

The kids were drunk. Sometimes they threw bottles at each other. Sometimes we got sprayed from the crashing bottles.

Sometimes the kids pissed into the sand. They were crazy kids. Girls and boys. And they couldn't see us where we perched.

It was hard not to laugh. We knew we could have scared them. We knew we could have jumped onto their backs. It scared us to think how we could scare them. We could have made them piss their pants.

But we liked the park.

So we held our breath.

We sat, silent, unmoving.

Some masks didn't work. These came back to the island in
dirty boxes. Some of the boxes were very small and crammed with
masks. The boxes were piled in the factory.

My father would blame the ladies.

You're not sewing them tight, he would say.

Peru would call. And Mexico.

Those days my father slammed his fist to the desk.

He stared at the pile of boxes.

He screamed for hours into the phone.

He would say, You're just not using them right.

Those days my brother watched the ladies work. I sat in the
lot with the goats. I waited for the husbands to wait for the ladies.

Mornings in Baltimore. Winter mornings. The curtain pierced
by a streak of light. And dust rode on the streak of light. And if I
waved my pillow the dust would scatter. I would choose a single dot
of dust. It would travel upward like a leaf in a storm. Like a single
snowflake in a gust of air. It would pass forever through space and
time. This speck of ancient human skin. The air was always full of
dust. And nothing could crush it.

On the ride to our dinner in the city my father said, Listen.

He talked of factories in foreign countries.

You don't want to know, he said.

But he at least made a filter to help.

He looked at me in the rearview mirror.

Sweatshops, he said. Now they can breathe.

He said, That's my job.

I looked out at the wilted highway palms.

He said, Listen.

In the rearview mirror he was eyes and eyebrows. A piece of forehead.

He said, There's dangerous dust all around us.

He said, My filter can crush the dust.

It's a killer, he said, pointing his hand like a gun at my brother's head.

The date picked dirt out from under her nails. Her nails were red and very long.

He said, Do me a favor.

He said, Please don't talk.

I'm not talking, I said.

He said, Shut your face.

He said, Don't even start.

Other drivers looked at us. Some were men. Their windows were open, their arms out the windows. Our windows were up.

My father said, What do you know about landfills.

But I wasn't thinking about the rats. About their sharp teeth chewing straight through the filters. The dangerous dust released.

I was watching a kid in the car next to ours. He was in the back seat like I was. He was watching me through the window too, but then he was gone.

My brother said nothing, reading his comic. We could hear his music.

My father said, What does she know. He looked at my brother. He said, Your sister's crazy. He laughed. He nudged my brother's arm.

My brother was off in his own crazy world. Who knew what he thought. His brain was made of dirt. Or shells. Or rotten fruit.

My father's forehead was sweating. The back of his neck was sweating. He said, You don't know shit. He smacked the wheel. He said, You just don't know.

There was dried grass all along the roadside. Signs for things. Drinks. Chickens, live and cooked.

He smacked the wheel. He said, What do you know.

Empanadas. Succulent ribs. Lemon-lime drink.

You know nothing, he said.

Homestyle empanadas. Like your mother's empanadas.

My mother made no empanadas.

We had regular food. American food.

Fried chicken in a bucket. Buttered rolls in a bucket. Regular drinks.

He said, Listen to me.

He said, You don't listen.

Then he slowly stopped the car in a lane on the highway. The date said something sad in Spanish. Cars screeched to a stop behind us. My father put the car into park. He got out of the car and walked into traffic.

In California my father rented a car and took us to theme parks. My brother and I rode the rides while my father sat on a bench drinking coffee from a paper cup.

At one park we could pan for gold. We left the park with vials of dirt. There were specks of gold in the dirt. It was hard to see the specks.

Hold that dirt, said my father.

You'll be rich, he said.

He took us to a restaurant, and the city blinked below us.

The wine made me feel like I could laugh. My brother's face was red.

My father said, This is the life.

I said, What do you mean.

I mean the life, he said.

Big deal, I said. And I knew that if I laughed my brother would start laughing too. And I knew that if my brother started that every person in the restaurant would turn and stare because my brother sounded like a retard, and now he was drunk as well.

So I held my breath and thought of my mother dying.

There was a time my father would say to me, One day it's yours.

I would take over. The men would work for me. The ladies too.

But the rats, I would say.

So my brother could take over instead. My brother the genius who couldn't tie a shoe.

The kids who came to the park at night were drunk. They were the wild kind of kids. They threw bottles and hard. They were looking for a fight. They could have killed us you know.

I imagine your father lying there on that street and how I would think what a fuckup, your father, and I would tell you this, and maybe we would laugh together over a drink and I would confess to you that my father, too, was a fuckup.

But it was my father lying in the street like that, and so I'm kind of alone here, you see, because your father, though maybe a fuckup in his own fucked up way, is not the fuckup mine is.

Your father would never have been there, and you know it, and we will never have a drink and laugh it up.

We were sitting, the three of us, in a lane on the highway. On a Friday of all days. Car horns blaring. Cars swerving around us. It was me and the date in the back seat. My brother's music went all the way up. My father was walking along the shoulder. Then he shrunk out of sight. A goat was walking along the shoulder. My brother saw the goat and laughed. Cars were nearly hitting us. I don't have to tell you how fast they were going. Our car shook when the others passed. It occurred to me to drive the car. But I didn't know how to drive yet. My father's date was crying. I wasn't old enough to drive. I said to the date, Drive the car. I wasn't nice in how I said it. Her shoulders were shaking. She looked so stupid. Like a stupid kid. Her shoulders shook from crying. I said, Drive-o the fucking car-o. I pointed to the steering wheel. I made my hands like I was driving. I yanked on her arm. I screamed, Drive-o drive-o. She climbed over into the driver's seat. I looked at her ass when she climbed over. Her pants were tight and pink. My brother moved his head to his music. He laughed but he couldn't hear himself laugh. He couldn't hear how stupid he sounded, how fucking retarded, and I can't even tell you what it did to me when he laughed like this. What it did to me in my gut. I said, Stop it you retard. Stop it you retard fucker. Look, he couldn't hear me. And he wasn't retarded. He was wired wrong. And we were about to be killed and it wasn't by our own choosing. The date drove slow and found my father walking. The goat was walking with him. Minutes we crept beside the two. My father walking rigid. His face and neck were red. The goat bounced beside him. The cars behind us nearly slammed us. I screamed at my brother to roll down his window. I took his headphones off his ears. I screamed again. Then my brother was crying. I screamed at my father to get in the car. I said to the date, Stop that crying el stupid-o bitch-o. The cars behind us nearly killed us. The goat ran into brown weeds off the highway.

I imagine my father laughs at some point, lying there on his back, facing nothing, the sky, and who knows what it looked like, the sky, that night, and, really, who cares.

I imagine, too, he had a bit too much to drink, and suddenly the whole thing seems very funny to my father, lying there, a fucking genius, an inventor for fuck's sake, his back pressed to the street.

Then he tries to move his arms to get himself up and the pain moves in faster than he can lift his body from the ground and he starts thinking it's not really so funny anymore, this life, the utter absurdity of it all, this life, I mean, really, the minute by minute tedious choice between pain and death.

Is this too much.

On the low-lit street the date ran like hell. She didn't come in to work the next morning.

She left me there, my father said.

My father and I sat at the table. No one was eating. My brother sat on the floor.

Pow, said my father.

Brass knuckles, he said.

And, he said, he has my wallet.

And he really socked me good.

My brother laughed.

My father looked over at my brother.

My father said, Is something funny.

My brother was laughing on the floor.

My father got up and walked toward my brother. My brother's sneakers were cockeyed, the Velcro undone.

My father was staring, noticing something.

I said, Don't stare.

He said, Tie your shoes, son.

But there were no ties.

He said, Did you hear me, son.

He walked closer to my brother.

My brother back-crept to a corner.

My father said, You think this is funny.

He said, You think it's funny that your father got socked.

My brother laughed. I knew he was laughing at the word socked. I knew he would think this word was funny. And my father said it thick and slurred. It sounded more like thocked. And that was funny.

My father said, What's funny, son.

I said, Did you thock him back.

My father turned to look at me. His eyelids were swollen.

Who do you think you are, he said.

You should have thocked him, I said.

My father's nose was bleeding again.

My brother was laughing his head off.

My father turned to my brother.

I picked up the pitcher.

You should have thocked him, I said.

My father turned. He said, You know nothing.

He said, Do yourself a favor. He said, Put that pitcher down.

You should have crushed him, I said.

I was standing by the table.

Then I was standing on a chair.

He said, Get off that chair.

My brother put his headphones on. He turned his music up. I could hear his music. Some metal song I had heard before. And I heard the ocean. Or was it the air. Something whistled. My brother's head rocked. Light came from the window. There were millions of dust specks in the light. I said, This place is fucking dusty. Then something crashed. Then something else.

As my father was getting back into the car he said to me, You don't know shit.

The date climbed into the back.

Drivers swore at us. My father drove. We ate somewhere in the city. Rice and beans. Plantains. Everything was soft and wet.

My brother read his comic. He wore his headphones.

The date looked at her lap. She was devout. A good one. But her pants were pink and up her crack. In the States she would have been another kind of lady. My brother and I saw this kind of lady when we took the long way home from the park. Some of the ladies were men. They called my brother Sugar. This made my brother laugh.

I should say, before I forget, that I liked the city. San Juan. Music came from every doorway. There were dogs on the sidewalks. Hookers on the sidewalks. Smells like the smell of burning meat.

On the ride home from dinner no one spoke. I sat as far from the date as I could. I pressed my face to the window and thought of my face pressed to the window. I thought of what it looked like from the other side. I thought of some kid in another back seat. How he would look at me with my face pressed tight. He would know I was stupid and from the States. He would know I couldn't climb a palm. I couldn't split a coconut. I liked American coconut shredded in a bag. Hamburgers on rolls. Kentucky Fried. And I thought of the goat who ran into weeds. And I thought of how to find the goat. And if I found the goat of what I would do. I would treat it like it was a dog.

I don't believe there was a man in a ski cap. I think the date punched my father in the face. I think the date's husband punched my father in the face. I think a hooker punched my father in the face. I think a wild kid stabbed my father in the face. I think a lady driver ran over my father's face. I think a Coco Loco split open my father's face. I think the concierge shot my father in the face. I think the goats bit my father's face. I think the rats chewed my father's face. I think the ghost of my mother punched my father in the face. I think my brother laughed in my father's face. I think I threw a pitcher at my father's face. I threw a pitcher at my father's face. I was aiming for my father's face. My father ducked. I threw a pitcher at the wall behind my father.

My brother was the one called retarded in school, and I was the one who punched the kids who called him retarded.

My brother could say the alphabet backward and he could count backward and he could do other things that I couldn't do. And I wasn't stupid. So he wasn't retarded.

There was a night, late, my father out, my brother and I sneaked to the beach. We saw kids on the beach and a fire burning. The Coco Locos and their friends around a fire.

When they saw us they screamed out, America.

They said, Stupid fucks.

But they laughed so we walked even closer.

A radio on the sand played fast-speed music. Some kids danced in the sand by the fire. Sparks from the fire scared my brother. He looked like he was about to cry. He started to back-creep to the hotel. I felt that weirdness in my gut. But before I could call him a fucking retard, and before someone else could call him a retard, and before I could punch that person in the face, someone, a girl, held my brother's arm. Next thing my brother was walking toward the fire. Next he was dancing on the sand. I have to say he danced like a retard. It wasn't his kind of music.

And there was a night my brother and I walked home from the city park. The street was unlit and we were the only ones. A car slowed beside us. We kept on walking. It was Baltimore and we knew how to get home. The car crept along and we walked a bit faster. The window went down. The man said, Get in, and we ran.

And I always wondered, years after the man slowed his car and said, Get in, where we might have gone had we gotten in.

My father stood with a fork in one hand. A glass in the other. Blood dripped into his mouth.

There was bread on the floor. Fruit on the floor. Splinters of glass and broken dishes. Egg yolk stuck to the walls. To my arms.

I was still standing on the chair.

The silver pitcher had rolled back and back and back then stopped.

My brother went to the factory. The ladies would give him pan de agua. They would call him Sweetie and play with his hair.

I don't know how long we stood like that.

My father picked up the pitcher.

I don't need to say how fucked up it was.

My father said, Who do you think you are.

I was taller on the chair. I was crazy, monstrous, on the chair.

I said, Who do you think you are.

The pitcher had hit the wall behind him. It was all fucked up. I don't need to say how dented.

My father said, I know who I am.

I wanted to see myself on the pitcher. It was all dented now. I wanted to see what the pitcher could do.

My father said, You know who I am.

I could have jumped him from the chair. I could have made him piss his pants.

I'm a genius, he said.

I could have crushed him to bits.

I'm your father, he said.

My brother could hang upside-down on the monkey bars and the blood never rushed to his head.

He could jump off the monkey bars and land on his knees or his face or his back and not cry.

So he was the one to jump off the monkey bars that one time, that last time we went to the park. He was the one to land on those kids and I was the one laughing my ass off.

And on the monkey bars that last time, I remember thinking, Don't do it, because I could feel what he was about to do.

And I remember thinking, Do it already, because who knows why. I just did.

My mother had already died. My father was moving around the house. He was putting things into boxes and bags. He was trashing his failed inventions. None worked the way they should have worked. We were leaving for the summer for the island.

So that one time, the last time we went to the park, my broth-er jumped onto those kids.

And I can't tell you how scared those kids were. I mean they nearly died. They never saw it coming. I just laughed my ass off. And at that moment I felt very alive. And I knew that I was very alive. And I knew that the moment would pass. And that's how I knew I was very alive and that living was the step before not living. I mean that living was the step before dust. And dust was some crazy kind of eternal. And the whole world felt crazy, and I was laughing too hard. And before I fell from laughing so hard I was yanked down from my perch. And we both got punched and punched and punched. And it was worth it.

But every time before that time we sat there silent, unmov-ing.

At home my mother drifted in and out of what was next.

My father, the TV blue on his face, half-slept on the edge of a chair.

Below the kids pissed onto the swings.

The kids made out in the sand.

The city blinked like stars.

And when the sky was blackest and the kids left the park, my brother and I jumped down from our perch and walked the long way home.

The Walk

there's the ceiling, the ceiling fan spinning dust, the bed undone underneath, and you're in the bed waking, no, you're always awake when it's this hot, this late, the ceiling fan humming, spinning dust in the dark, then in daylight, its motor a car sound, an idling, a bus sound humming, the fan blades stirring, sweat streaking the bed and the streaks widen, stain, your eyes closed tight, and the room seems outside, open, a bus motor idling, the spin of leaves and rain, a school trip in fall, standing curbside on Lexington near Lexington Market, standing lightheaded in the yellow glare of raincoats, in the hum of the buses, in the squeal on the streets made of glass, they are, said your father, again and again, made of glass, and they glitter, and you need to be inside, shut in the school bus, warm in the bus where your teeth won't chatter, where your skin won't creep, where you're sheltered, clearheaded, and you open your eyes and you're inside, waking, no, always awake, and it's no longer morning and the rain is sweat, the leaves are heat, the yellow raincoats dull to hot air, an undone bed, black shoes in the corner, the black like a pit, like a hole to a cave where you can't hear the fan, where you can't hear it spin, when in Baltimore and in summer, when on Fayette Street, when the phone rings the head throbs, don't answer the phone now, it's time for a walk, when you're ready to stand, you're not ready, get ready,

the pills soften in the throat and the water comes late, warm in the glass, leaving a taste everyone knows as white, aspirin, and white is bitter everyone knows, even your father said, don't chew, swallow, bitter, aspirin, and the pills will kick in, not yet, in an hour, aspirin takes an hour, from noon to one, and you float through the room, slip out of clothing, slip into clothing, under the fan pushing dust, its motor humming, and you hold your black shoes, one in each hand, you float to the window, it's open already, Baltimore shimmering through the window in a haze, Howard Street, Lexington, Calvert, Charles, made of what, said your father, glass, you said, and it glitters in the light, in the white haze of summer, as you drop your black shoes from the window to the walk, and the black shoes will wait for you on the walk, and your hands are free and you can hold air solid, cloudy, on a finger, in a hand, in the crook of an arm, as the phone rings, let it, and the air feels like foam, like sap, squeezed tight in a fist, in the crook of the neck, and below are your shoes curled on the walk, turned to their sides, crooked like what, like pain, no, like laughing, it's funny, and you can't reach the shoes as you live on the top floor and heat rises, everyone knows, even your father said so when you had a fever, when the school bus took you from Lexington Market to in front of your house and you saw the sign for 30th Street, where you ate and slept, where you lived with your mother, your father, where you fell lightheaded to the wet leaves and grass, heavyheaded you had fallen face first to the wet, fainted, said your father as he ran outside, his word riding on a cloud to bring you to, to bring you in, and the heat rose to your head from your wrist and your father said, fever, gave aspirin and ice and covers and you slept, you waked, you slept, you waked,

the glass of water shatters to the walk, to Baltimore, to the shoes on the walk, it was an accident, the glass was wet and slipped, and the water in the glass was warm anyway, and the grass jutting up through cracks in the walk needs the water anyway when there's never rain, not even a spray or mist to break the heat, not even a raincloud, and the water was warm anyway in the glass from the sun throbbing low through the window, and you can hear the sun sounding like a pulse but it's a pulsing in your head, blood pulsing in your wrist, and you can see the blood-pulse jump in one wrist, now the other, as your arms hang limp in the sap, as they hang out the window, and looking at your pulse is looking at your life in slow-motion, how you will always be this, this, this, how your life and the sun are the same pulse-throb throbbing, and your father called you blue-blood from the veins in a wrist, blue-blooded from fainting, he took your pulse, you took an aspirin, don't chew, then covers, ice on your wrist, then quiet, sleep, car sounds in sleep, dreams of fights, of car horns blaring on 30th Street, and you waked in the same place, in the same bed, to your sponge-faced mother, another aspirin, water, Lexington Market still afloat in your head like clouds, like rain, the crabs sideways crawling in wet glass boxes, the birds strung up with blood-soaked rope, the cows staring blankly behind small windows, the buzzing of lights and the smell of food was it, or slaughter you could say today, was it slaughter, the blood, and you wondered of the cows, why everyone laughed in their yellow raincoats and yellow boots, they laughed at what happened behind the small windows, the cows were back there blankly staring, you turned your back to their stares, your front to the scattered raincoats like all the suns burning your eyes when you opened your eyes in Lexington Market, on Lexington Street, on the bus going homeward, on the grass at home, inside with fever to take an aspirin, how you opened your eyes at noon today, in this place, Baltimore, St. Paul Street, Fayette Street, word-named streets, where the buildings shimmer in a sun haze, where the sun seems stuck up there like in glue or in a spread of white plaster, where the shoes on the walk look disfigured, distorted through the heat like shadows of crabs crawling up St. Paul, Fayette, and the heat floats you from the window,

the heat floats you to the darkest room to its darkest corner and you find yourself standing barefoot in the kitchen, you find yourself standing crooked, useless, and it's funny to be barefoot in a kitchen when you almost remember like a dream of what was it when you see your bare feet pressed to the floor and realize there is no one, was there ever, when you were younger with fever, you were sheltered, now you're older with veins in your bare feet, blue blood running through your hot feet, you're older, you're this-old this-old this-old, like twenty like thirty, and the kitchen is dark, the freezer is empty, just ice and cold air, no longer a cave like when your father gave ice, he said, go back to bed you have fever, and, no more Lexington Market for you, and, you can't handle these trips to the market, and you looked in the freezer when you were burning cold-hot and your father said, climb in it's a cave to cool you, and it looked like a cave of frozen dirt, of scratchings on walls of cows and trees, climb in, said your father, but you were already too big and if you could have made yourself smaller, if you could now, if you could crawl inside and curl and sleep like a bear in a cave, the pills will kick in in an hour, who said an hour, someone said, it's only aspirin, your father said, one hour, he said, you'll be fine by tomorrow, though they don't always kick in, aspirin, and what is the magic of an hour when your head is splitting from no sleep, from heat, what is the magic of timing time when you're always looking to the end, when you always need the other side of an hour, when the other side is sixty minutes away and when you get sixty minutes away you are sixty minutes older and sixty minutes older, when you're lucky, when you're not, when you're lucky,

the staircase is soundless, bare feet are silent, thank goodness, when you're throbbing, splitting, and the shoes are waiting there for you on the walk, and the door shuts behind you and you're outside, shoeless, sweating, squinting upward to your window, and it's hard to believe you live behind that window where the fan spins slowly on the ceiling and it seems it should do more, all that life, it should sound more like a bear, less like a motor,

when your father said, go to sleep, you asked of the cows and your father said, sleep, you slept, you heard a motor in your head, a fighting fever-dream, awake in an hour, screaming for your father, the fever unbroken, the dream fading out like a day, almost forgotten, another aspirin, your wrung-out mother saying, swallow,

the phone is still ringing, your father calling from someplace, outside, Florida, but you can't rush inside, it's too hot, you can't rush in to answer, and it's just your father from outside by his car, the motor running, in that place, Florida, saying, hello blue-blood, as he said when you were hazy from fever, he said, come back blue-blood, when you were out there in a fever-dream, burning like summer, when your head was sap, as the sky gets in summer, when

your head was a cow's head, blood-rushed and hot, pressed heavy
to the wet leaves and grass,

you're standing shoeless near curled shoes and funny to throw your
shoes from the window so they could curl in the sun, but the staircase was soundless, goodness, and what right shoes curl from heat,
what right shoes crab-crawl on the walk and who said to crash the
glass to your shoes, your only glass, but that was an accident, and
you're standing shoeless on the shards, an accident, and your foot
is bleeding, an accident, really, who can think on a white-hot day
in Baltimore in a sun haze with a throbbing split-up head like with
fever, like when your father said, come back, he thought he lost you
to fever, isn't this right, it doesn't seem right when there you were in
the same bed in the same room in the same house on 30th, waking
in an hour to your dried-up mother by the same bed in the same
room, just your mother in the room saying, swallow, when your
father went, is that right, it wasn't that day was it but another, it
wasn't that day was it when he left, don't think it was that day when
you were fainted from fever and really can't remember,

when the fever broke you walked to the kitchen and your mother
stood withered, barefoot, looking at the window and it was already
funny to be barefoot in a kitchen and you looked in the freezer
and it was just a freezer, no longer a cave but dim walls and cold
air, how it's dim walls and cold air on this word-named street in
this same old city on this glaring hazy day today when the sky is so
thick and white you can't see clouds floating and you have to ask if
anything is still afloat,

it's time, just a walk around the corner, just some air, and you
should turn and walk before someone looks from your window, but
there's no one, just the phone, but you should walk before someone

calls from your window, but really there's no one, you're grown now, you're thirty, you're twenty, you're nineteen eighteen fourteen thirteen, you're nineteen, you're thirty, you should turn and walk before you rush back inside, before you answer the phone, before your father says, hello blue-blood, how's Baltimore blue-blood, can you see the glass streets from your window, can you see Lexington Market from where you live, can you see the crabs sideways crawling in watery cases, can you see the cows' heavy staring and the birds strung up with rope, and he would never say this, but if he did, but he wouldn't, but if he did you would tell him you can see the whole market shimmer from your window and you can smell the crabs, the sand and salt, the blood of the cows, you can hear their blood pulsing when the air is thinner, when the sky is bluer, you can see the window in the market from your window and the cows' heads past the window about to hit the straw floor, the cement floor, and you can see the laughing yellow raincoats, you can see how funny it is to be on the good side of a window and the cows can see you laughing and laughing because you can take it now because you really don't care now because you're grown now, this old, and the cows can see their last see-through and it's you there laughing it up before their heads hit the floor before their time is up,

when the fever broke you walked to the kitchen and your mother stood tired, barefoot, looking out the window, and your father walked in wet-haired, withered, goodness, that day, you remember that day, he'd only been out for a walk,

listen, the phone's still ringing behind your window and listen, the fan's still spinning behind your window and look, the sky's a white glare in your window and look, the sun's a white haze in the sky in your window and look, there's oil from your eyes and salt from your eyes floating like hairs on the sun in your window and look, there's blood on the walk hot under your feet before you slip on your shoes, before you turn to walk,

The Garage

We saw the two cars in the garage. The ladder lay on its side. There were rusted paint cans by the wall. Paintbrushes stuck to the tops of the cans. Brooms poked up from a bucket. The ladder lay between the two cars. The brooms cast a shadow like the shadow of a man.

We saw milk crates scattered across the floor. We saw jump ropes, skates. These were ours. On the floor were open magazines. The pages flapped from the breeze that came in. The light was on above our heads. The garage door was shut tight before we raised it. We were not supposed to raise the door. Our mother always told us to keep from the garage. Our father was not one to give a damn.

The magazines popped opened to their centers. They were magazines we were not supposed to see. The ladder lay between the two cars. No, it leaned against a car. It leaned against the coupe. The coupe was the car our father drove. Our mother drove the wagon.

The ladder was broken, rotted. Its rungs were split. The milk crates are what he climbed that day. The milk crates were ours.

Our mother walked to work that morning. She worked at the synagogue doing something. The synagogue was in the next neighborhood. Some days, if the weather was nice, she walked. On this day the weather seemed nice enough. Though it looked a little like it could rain. We thought we heard thunder in the distance.

The garage door was painted blue. Same as the shutters on the house. Same as the front door. The dark shade of blue our mother chose standing at the counter in the paint store when we were smaller and waiting by the paint store door with our father who, our mother had decided, would paint the house before the summer turned too warm. Our mother bought the ladder that day in the paint store. She bought rollers and brushes and a blue shade of paint. Our father leaned back, his back to the door.

Our mother was careful not to park the wagon too close to the coupe in the garage. The wagon doors could have scratched the coupe. And then what.

In the dark hallways at school there was no one to catch us walking into school late. There were no teachers in the hallways handing out slips. This was junior high. The bells were ringing. So no one noticed when we slipped into our first classes so late the classes were ending.

There was a metal hoop above the garage door, rusted in places, bent. A net hung from the hoop by a single weathered loop of string. A basketball lay deflated in the yard, stuck in the weeds. Our mother often said on her quick walk from the wagon to the front door, looking at the rusted hoop, looking at the deflated ball in the weeds, You kids can't take care of anything, and, Lord give me strength.

The synagogue had stained glass windows. We sat in the row of hard seats in the back. This, despite our mother's protests. This, despite her, You'll sit up front with me, I'll be the laughingstock, Damn you kids. The synagogue ladies had enormous tits. They said to our mother, Let them sit in the back.

We should not have been in the garage. But we never cared what our mother told us. We hid our skates and jump ropes, the magazines, in a corner in dusty milk crates. We took our things out of hiding after school. Mostly when there was rain. Or when nothing good was on TV.

Minutes dragged at school that day, as they did on others, but even more slowly that day, the long second hands of the clocks just dragging across the clocks' faces. And we tried, in our separate classrooms, for we were in separate grades with separate teachers, to hold our breath for thirty seconds just to see if we could, watching the hands drag along the faces. But we could not hold our breath for more than twenty seconds, as twenty seconds, when holding our breath, felt longer than a minute, felt longer even than an hour, and we took in air at twenty seconds, trying not to be heard by anyone around us, knowing we would tell each other in the lunchroom, as we did every day, how long we held our breath in class.

There was a string tied to the bell that hung from the paint store door we could not help but shake to make the bell jingle, until our father told us to keep our hands in our pockets, saying the one who did so for longest could ride shotgun in the wagon and push the button to raise the garage door when we pulled into the drive.

In the synagogue were twenty rows of seats. We counted them from our place in the back. The rabbi confused us when we listened. He looked at us as he talked. We were the stars that day.

When our father bought the coupe he insisted on fully equipped, despite our mother's protests. She said, Your father thinks he's a kid, and slammed a door. They had made a deal though. If he painted the house the blue she wanted, he would get a new coupe at the end of summer. He would get it fully equipped.

Our mother used to make us go to the synagogue on Saturdays. Our father stayed home and watched TV. We did not want to go with our mother. We wanted to watch TV instead. Or go for a ride with our father. Our mother said, I'll be the laughingstock. Our father never looked up from the TV. Our mother went out to the wagon. Our father said, Your mother thinks she cares. We did not know what he meant. Our mother blared the horn. Our father never looked up. In the wagon we held our breath in the back seat. Our mother did not care if we held our breath.

Our father found the milk crates where we hid our things in a corner of the garage. He dumped our things out of the milk crates, scattering the things across the floor. We wondered if our father wondered why our things, which should have been in our bedrooms, were in milk crates in the garage. And we wondered if he wondered what the magazines were doing there. The magazines were his.

But our father, most likely, did not even blink, did not even wonder why our things were in the milk crates in the garage. He, most likely, did not even notice that the magazines from beneath his side of the bed were in the milk crates as he turned them over. Our father carried the milk crates to the space between the cars. He stacked the milk crates and stood on the stack. The ladder leaned against the coupe in a way that likely scratched it.

This is really a story about our father. About how he hanged himself in the garage that day. We used to say he hung himself. But the word is hanged.

A neighborhood kid had told us of someone who could breathe through his eyes and so we both tried to breathe through our eyes but could not. We knew if we could breathe through our eyes, we would give the appearance of holding our breath for hours. We practiced this in class for it was something to do to pass the time. But we could only hold our breath for twenty seconds and never breathed through our eyes. We were trying to get to thirty seconds. We thought that perhaps if we got to thirty without breathing, our eyes would have to start to breathe. We started when the second hand reached twelve. We knew if we tried to do this every time the hand reached twelve, we would do this fifty times a class. And the class would go by faster. The hands just dragged around the faces. This day we felt the sickening gray wave. Only when we were breathing. Only when the hand passed near the six, seven, eight, and we were taking in air like the other kids. Only when we were breathing steady, not thinking of not breathing. This day we felt the most sickening gray wave, the wave we felt often enough, though never did we feel this sick. We had watched our father from the sticker bushes through the window after one of their fights. We often watched him through the window. But this time he sat at the kitchen table for longer than he should have. This time he rubbed his face at the table, late for work. We were late for school.

We could never sit still in the synagogue. We did not understand the rabbi's words. We ran down the aisle. We hid in the coatroom. The synagogue ladies yelled, Enough. Our mother never took us for ice cream after. We always rode home in the back seat. We stared out of opposite windows. We said, You never take us for ice cream. Our mother pushed the garage door button. She parked the wagon, said, Your father and his toys, making sure not to hit the coupe.

We played horse after dinner in summers in the drive. All the neighborhood kids came over. The sun went low behind our house. The coupe thundered up the street. We made way for the coupe in the drive. Dad's home, we said. The kids knew to back up into the yard. The basketball got tossed to somewhere. Everyone stood in the yard somewhere to make room for the coupe. Game over, we said.

The rabbi said, There are signs and meanings. He looked at us. We knew of signs and meanings, but we did not know what the rabbi meant.

One day we begged our father for a ride. Our father was doing nothing that day but watching TV. It was Saturday. Our mother had gone to the synagogue. We no longer had to go. Our father was still unshaven. He had purple pouches beneath his eyes. We said to our father, You never take us for a ride, knowing he would cave, knowing he would take us, saying, Get in the coupe already, One up front, One in back. We fought it out, both of us calling shotgun. The coupe was no longer new. Still, it went fast. Still, it went faster than the wagon. It went faster than other cars on the road. We screamed, Faster, faster, when we reached the hilly parts, hoping we would fly off the hills and bump our heads on the roof of the coupe when we landed. We screamed, Slow down, as we neared the toy store, begging our father to pull into the lot and park and let us walk through the store, promising him we would not ask for toys, we would not touch a thing, promising no hysterics when we walked out with nothing new in our hands.

We sat in the lunchroom thinking whether or not we should leave through the back door as we sometimes did, thinking whether or not we should go home and watch TV or play broom hockey in the half of the garage that was always empty in the daytime, the half where our father would park the coupe later that night when he got home from work, tired, way past dinner.

One rule to follow when walking through the toy store was, Look but don't touch, even if there were toys we wanted, ones we'd seen on TV when watching TV after school. One rule was, Keep your hands in your pockets, even if we had no pockets, and we understood what this meant and kept our hands by our sides. One rule was, Don't ask for anything, and we knew we were not supposed to ask for anything, but often we did, often going into fits of hysterics when we were told no, often pulling our hands from our pockets and touching everything we could.

We wanted our mother to drive us to school. One of us said, It looks like rain. We thought we heard thunder. And our mother said, You won't drown. Our parents were having a fight. Our mother said, Take your keys. We wore our keys on strings around our necks. We chewed the strings during class.

The synagogue ladies taught us signs and meanings. They said a loose eyelash meant one could make a wish. A ringing in the ear meant one was being talked about. An itching in the palm meant one would get money. Aching in the legs meant a storm was on its way. They taught us to throw salt over our shoulders. So at dinners we spilled the salt on the tables. They screamed at us that enough was enough. But we shook salt from the shakers onto the floors. And we knocked on wood, we knocked on it hard, on their good tabletops, on the backs of chairs, and as hard as we could, until they called for our mother, said, Enough's enough.

The milk crates were stacked behind the junior high. We took them one day on our way home from school. We wanted to hide our things in the milk crates. We stacked them in a corner of the garage. No one ever looked in the corners.

We found our father leaning against the coupe in the parking lot of the toy store. He was looking off into who knows what. We said, Can we have something, and our father said, Not today. And we said, Why not, and our father said, Because I said so, and we said, We'll pay you back, and our father said, You have no money, laughing, saying, You have nothing, but we were almost in junior high and we said, We can get the money, and he said, You have nothing, but he was looking at who knows what. The sky.

It was hard to tell why they were fighting. Our father said

something. Our mother said, What do you care. They thought we had already gone to school. But really we were hiding in the sticker bushes out front, watching their fight through the window. We saw our mother hurl her car keys across the kitchen. They just missed hitting our father's face. Our father had ducked just in time. He said something. She said, What do you care. Our father said, Wait. But she left the house. We ducked lower in the bushes, laughing. Our mother was running down the drive. We looked through the window to see our father hurl a plate to the front door. He sat at the kitchen table. He rubbed his face. The pouches beneath his eyes looked darker. He was not crying. We felt the gray wave and stopped laughing.

But, really, it seems like none of this ever happened.

In the lunchroom one of us folded a piece of paper into a fat triangle, and one of us pushed it toward the other, and the other pushed it back, and so on, until the lunchroom bell rang, and we had just two classes left before we could walk home. We were no longer thinking of our father sitting at the kitchen table that morning, which seemed days ago already, really, all those minutes in a day, our father sitting there, the darkest pouches beneath his eyes, rubbing his just-shaved face. Really, it seemed like it never happened.

The synagogue ladies made us dinners. They lived in houses by the synagogue. We liked the neighborhood kids, not the synagogue kids. And the synagogue kids did not like us back. And the synagogue ladies did not like us either. They clattered in their kitchens making food for us that smelled bad. Chopped liver. Deviled eggs. Gefilte fish. The ladies pulled our faces toward their tits every chance they got and squeezed us. We were the stars that month. They sent cakes and briskets and boiled potatoes to the house. All this food filling the goddamn house.

We knew to hold our breath in the toy store when we did not get what we wanted. Our faces turned purple when we held our breath. Our mother could walk off when we did this. Our father could not walk off. He said we would faint. But we never fainted. And he always caved.

In our last class of the day we held our breath for almost twenty-two seconds straight. The second hand dragged from twelve to five. We let in air before it hit five. The teachers' voices sounded underwater. We felt we were slipping to the floor. The teachers never noticed us slipping. We hoped to last all the way to six. We wanted to drown out the teachers for longer. But the final bell rang.

In the paint store our mother held strips of colored paper. The strips were different shades of blue for she said she wanted a dark blue shade. Like midnight blue, she said to the paint store salesclerk, sending the three of us to the door to wait. The salesclerk handed her several strips of blue colored paper over the counter, and our mother walked to where we stood by the door waiting for her with our father, our hands in our pockets, strips of blue paper in her hand. She said to our father, What do you think, knowing he would not give a damn one way or the other, knowing how he never cared, Blue, green, red, What's the goddamn difference. She waved the paper strips in front of his face and said, What do you think. He looked at the strips and said, it turned out, I was thinking red.

We played a game of horse in the drive. The sun went low behind our house. We could hear our father's coupe in the distance.

Everyone backed into the yard. The coupe thundered up the drive. Our father blared the horn. The garage door wheezed upward. Our father pulled the coupe into the garage. He stepped out from the coupe and gave a look. A lost look. A look to the sky. A blank baby look we saw. A sign of trouble we now know. A look we could see was frightening, blank.

We dragged our father back inside the toy store. The basketball hoop was on a shelf. We said, Just look at it. The other customers looked at us. The salesclerk looked to see if our father would cave. We said, You never get us anything, and held our breath. Our father said to stop. He said, Whoever stops can push the button. But we were almost in junior high and no longer cared about pushing a button, raising a door. We held our breath. Our father caved. He said, I'll look if you stop, Lord help me.

Our mother answered the phone when the neighbor called her at work that afternoon. We could hear our mother's voice through the phone. The neighbor told her to hurry. We stood in the doorway of the neighbor's house. We heard our mother.

Our father was up on the ladder when it was a new ladder when we were small. Our father painted the shutters midnight blue, using the new brushes our mother bought in the paint store. He whistled some song and the shutters looked dark, too dark, and we knew our mother would think this.

We stood inside the synagogue ladies' houses in the terrible house smells that never smelled like our house but smelled like chopped liver and gefilte fish and piss and dog, no matter how nice the house was. We heard the kids upstairs in their bedrooms watching TV. These kids were not our friends. Our friends were the neighborhood kids. The synagogue kids were the kids our mother wanted us to play with. They all had TVs in their rooms. They always hid upstairs in their bedrooms watching TV until dinner was on the table. We heard their mothers talking to the kids and the kids saying things like, We're not friends, and the mothers shushing them, and the kids saying things like, I don't like them, and the mothers saying, Get dressed and get the hell downstairs.

On the walk home from school we dragged our feet. We dragged our jackets along the walk. It could have been any fall day, the dusty smell of leaves and cold. A smell of rain. Thunder in the distance. The airless basketball was still in weeds in the yard. Like a pumpkin growing there. A flattened out pumpkin. A good thought to have in fall. We did not want to watch TV that day. There was nothing worth watching besides. We wanted to look at magazines in the garage. We raised the garage door partway and saw the two cars. We dropped our jackets to the drive. We could not do anything with two cars there. We considered basketball, a game of horse. The two of us. The neighborhood kids had stopped coming around. We ran back to the airless ball in the weeds. Like picking a rotted out pumpkin. Water squeezed out from its air hole. We went to look for the air pump. It was weird in the daytime to see both cars. We never saw the coupe on a school day. We knew our mother walked to work. We saw her run off in the morning. It was not too far for her to walk. But not our father with some kind of work downtown. He always got home way past dinner. Meat warmed on a plate in the oven, potatoes. We thought, split second, our father stayed home sick. We remembered him rubbing his face that morning. We thought of checking in our parents' bedroom. We split second thought of waking him with a jump on the bed, something he would not have liked, perhaps, if sick, but still.

We raised the garage door higher. We saw the ladder. The rusted paint cans. The paintbrushes stuck to the tops of the cans. The brooms in a bucket. The milk crates scattered. The jump ropes, skates. The magazines. The light was on above us.

Look. There was a shadow. A shapeless shadow. It was not of the brooms. It was shaped like nothing and cast on the cars. This does not sound right. But look. We looked up.

The salesclerk in the toy store said, You lucky kids. We looked at the purple pouches beneath our father's eyes. The salesclerk said, You lucky ducks, A brand new basketball hoop for you and a brand new ball. Plus a new air pump. We knew the salesclerk hated us. She hated how we acted. She wanted to smack us. We could tell.

The rabbi said that those in hell had their arms stuck out in front. He said that in hell they could not bend their arms at the joints. There were tables and tables of food in hell, all the wonderful food you could imagine. He said this food was there for everyone to eat, and that was hell.

The front door swung open. Our mother came outside to inspect our father's work. Our father never said, What do you think. Our mother blocked the sun with one hand and cried. She said, Shit. She said to us, crying, It's too goddamn dark, and our father, regardless, bought the coupe.

On the ride home from the toy store neither of us called shotgun. Both of us chose to sit in the back seat where we could flick the back of our father's neck for fun as he tried to drive. We laughed at this, at our flicking his neck until our father said, Stop it.

So we stopped. But then we leaned up and flicked his neck again. Our father said, I told you to stop, so we stopped, sat back in the seat, then we leaned up slowly, looking at each other, both of us trying not to laugh, and flicked his neck. Our father pulled the coupe onto the shoulder and we stayed there. He said nothing. The traffic whooshed past.

The neighborhood kids backed into the yard. Our father stepped out from the coupe. He gave a look that was frightening, blank. He picked up the basketball from the yard. He stood with the ball in his hands. He hurled the ball at a neighborhood kid. He said, Get the fuck out of my way. The ball rolled into the weeds. Game over. The kids ran home. We ran into the house. Our mother was watching our father from the window. Our father stood frozen in place in the yard. One of us said, What's wrong with Dad, and our mother said, He's just in a mood.

The day our father brought the new coupe home, our mother told us never to touch the outside, never to eat inside it, never to play in or around it, never to leave trash on its floor. That goes for you too, she said to our father. She said to us, He thinks he's a kid. Our father made room in the garage for the coupe, moving the ladder, the paint cans, the brushes out from the garage and into the backyard. Our mother said, There's room in the garage for everything, We just bought that ladder, We just bought those brushes. Our mother tried to bring the things back into the garage, but our father said no. He said the things were just taking up space. He said he would bring it all to the curb on trash day. But our mother said why throw the things away. Our father said he would no longer be needing them. He said he was done with painting shutters and doors. Our mother said, You never know. She did not like the blue she chose. It was too dark. She would be the laughingstock. Our father said, Lord. Our mother slammed a door. The things went forgotten. They stayed in the backyard through fall and winter. Our mother brought them back into the garage in spring. The ladder looked rotted in places. The paint cans were rusted. Our father saw our mother from the window. He said, Are you crazy. And she said, You're crazy. She pushed the things to the wall of the garage.

When our father hammered in the new basketball hoop, all the neighborhood kids stood around watching, hoping he would not fall from the now-weathered ladder. No. We all hoped he would fall. We hoped he would slip from the now-weathered ladder as it creaked and swayed on his way up the brittle rungs. We hoped the ladder would collapse. We hoped he would collapse and fall to his face. We did not hope that he would die, but we hoped that he would crack his skull, that he would bleed a bit. And there would be sirens, a trip to the hospital, something to pass the time.

So we watched as our father hammered in the last nail and climbed down slowly, the ladder creaking with every step, the ladder swaying slightly, and no one moved to hold the swaying ladder to help him. We watched him take the last few steps downward, and it did not look good, we could tell it did not look good, and his shoes pressed straight through the brittle rungs, which broke like twigs beneath his shoes, so that he slid to the ground in a quick bump bump bump, the ladder collapsing, and he landed on his ass in the drive. All the kids laughed as he stood, shaking, as he picked up the basketball from the yard, as he took the first shot with the new ball, one handed, shaking, still, from the ladder collapsing, trying to laugh, and we could see this, how hard he was trying to laugh, and he missed the hoop by several feet, the ball rolling into the weeds to pick up dirt. Lord we laughed as he walked into the house, dirt on his ass, a split in his pants, walking hunched without removing the fallen ladder from the drive, without retrieving the ball from the weeds, all the kids in the yard laughing, our mother laughing from the window, still laughing when she dragged the broken ladder back into the garage and pulled the door shut.

Our father dragged the broken ladder to between the two cars, forgetting he had split the rungs some time ago, and upon seeing the split rungs, he let the ladder collapse to the coupe. It scratched the coupe. We can say that now. We saw a scratch.

Our father found the milk crates in a corner, dumped the contents of the milk crates, carried the milk crates to between the two cars, and stacked the crates and climbed them. He tied a rope around the pipes on the ceiling in the back of the garage. He tied the rope in the space where the door, when raised upward to open, did not overlap the ceiling.

It should have been our father sitting on the edge of a milk crate, the rope in his hand, reconsidering.

It should have been our father dropping the rope to the floor, deciding to go to work.

Our father did not think we would find him. He did not think we used the garage. He thought we would open the front door using the keys we wore on chewed strings around our necks. He thought we would step inside the house, we would drop our jackets to the floor, we would watch TV waiting for our mother, waiting for our dinner.

And he did not think our mother would find him. She walked to work and would not need to park her car in the garage. She would come in through the front door like we did. She would make our dinner, and the three of us would eat in front of the TV, our father's dinner warming in the oven. And then what.

Perhaps our mother would have called him at work. And perhaps someone there would have answered the phone and said, He didn't come in to work today. And perhaps she would have called the synagogue ladies a little worried as it had gotten late and as there seemed no good reason for him not to have gone in to work. And perhaps the ladies would have suggested calling the local hospitals, for maybe he slipped and fell or who knew what. And perhaps our mother would have called the local hospitals only to find out nothing. And perhaps the ladies would have suggested she drive the wagon around the neighborhoods looking for his car. And perhaps our mother, at this point, would only have been half-listening. Perhaps she would have been considering the possibility that he left her. Perhaps she would have been regretting already the terrible way she had treated him over the years. And perhaps we would have sensed her regret and perhaps we would have felt a similar regret from the terrible way we had treated our father over the years. And perhaps we would have silently vowed to act more caring in the future. Perhaps we would have made some kind of pact with God to act more caring around our father instead of being the perfect brats we had become. And perhaps had this happened, our father would have walked in from the rain, said, Sorry, traffic, and sat with us, waiting for his dinner.

Or perhaps our mother would have walked out the door and into the rain and into the garage to get the wagon to take it for a drive through the neighborhoods. And she would have seen the coupe in the garage. And she would have seen him in the garage. And then.

There was an afternoon siren. All the neighborhood kids came running to see. We stood in the yard. Our house looked blurred. The trees looked blurred. Lights spun in the blue shuttered windows. It felt weird with everyone standing in front of our house. The garage door was halfway up. Our mother came running up the street. She screamed his name, our names. She pushed a way through the crowd. Someone tried to cover our eyes. Someone dragged us by our arms to the walk. Our mother picked up the basketball from the drive. It looked like a big flat pumpkin. We wondered why she was squeezing the ball how she was. Water squirted from its air hole. Our mother threw the ball at us. She screamed, You can't take care of anything. The garage door wheezed downward. The crowd of neighbors stood on the walk. They whispered. Scattered. Our mother went into the house. The neighborhood kids walked home.

The rabbi said that those in heaven had their arms stuck out in front. He said that they, too, like those in hell, could not bend their arms at the joints. He said there were tables of wonderful food in heaven and this food was there for everyone to eat. He said to imagine the trouble you would face in heaven and in hell. He said to imagine you were starving and there was wonderful food on tables, but you could not eat the food because your arms were stuck out in front. He said to imagine you could lift the food with your hands but you could not get the food to your mouth with your arms unable to bend at the joints. He said, Wouldn't you suffer. He said, Wouldn't you starve. The rabbi said if you could imagine what this would feel like, to suffer, to starve, then you could imagine hell. For in heaven, no one suffered. For they knew to feed each other.

Someone in the lunchroom said he stood on a bucket. And when he was ready he kicked it out from beneath him. Do you get it, He kicked the bucket. But the bucket was in a corner. The bucket was filled with brooms.

Someone in the neighborhood said, They saw the legs first. Someone said, No, they saw the shoes. Someone said, No, they saw clothing piled on the floor. Not true. Someone said, No, they saw the shadow of the legs, And he wore no pants. Not true. He was fully clothed. Someone said, They saw his underwear first. Not true. He was not crazy. And someone said, Where were his hands, and someone said, On his thing. No. And someone said, Not both hands, one. And someone said, So where was his other. His arms were hanging by his sides. And someone said, There were magazines, Dirty ones. Yes. That part was true.

On the floor of the back seat of the coupe we found several knotted up ties. We wondered why our father would throw his ties to the floor knotted up like that. We said, We found your ties, sitting there on the shoulder, cars whooshing past. We were unsure of what to do with our hands.

Someone in the coatroom said, First they called the hospital, and someone said, No, first they called their mother, and someone said, No, first they called the neighbors, and someone said, No, first they ran to the neighbors', and someone said, No, first they checked his pulse. No, first we touched his legs. We were like, You touch him, No, you touch him, and we both touched his legs. And someone said, No, first they screamed and screamed, Can you imagine what it felt like to touch him, They just screamed and screamed. Then we ran outside. We ran down the drive. They fainted. We did not faint. We ran down to the walk. The basketball fell. The whole world spun. We stood at a neighbor's door.

Our father always ate dinner alone. He watched TV while he ate. Sometimes he wasn't looking at the TV. Sometimes he looked at the wall. We sometimes watched him eating his dinner from the sticker bushes out front. He ate very fast. Sometimes he had food on his tie. And sometimes he had food on his face. And this usually made us laugh.

On the shoulder, the traffic passed in a whoosh. It felt like the whole car lifted and settled every time a car whooshed past. We sat on the shoulder despite our crying, despite our begging, Let's go home now Dad. We tried to hold our breath. We hit the back of his head from the back seat. His head lay against the steering wheel.

We found the air pump beneath the coupe. Many things had rolled beneath the cars.

The rabbi held our hands in the coatroom. We wanted to leave. We wanted to get back to the house where there would be brisket and cake and casserole. We would try to eat with our arms stuck out in front. We would not need to feed each other. We knew better ways to do it. We could toss the food into the air and catch it in our mouths. We could eat straight from the casserole dishes. The rabbi told us to close our eyes. We did not close our eyes. He said for us to imagine heaven. He closed his eyes. He said to imagine our father was in heaven. He said something else. And something else. But we were no longer listening to what he was saying. We were looking at the clock on the wall behind him. We were holding our breath for going on thirty seconds.

One of the synagogue kids said, Well, why did he do it, and
the kid's mother said, Go to your room, and the kid said, Why
should I, and the mother said, And don't come out, putting her
arm around our mother's back, and the kid said, Why, and one of
us said, What do you care. The kid said, But why, and the mother
said, Perfect brat, and, Do you want a smack, and our mother said,
It's fine, really, and one of us said to the kid, What do you care,
and the kid said, Was he crazy, and the mother said, I said to go
to your room, and the kid said, Well, was he crazy, and one of us
said, Fuck you, fucker, and our mother said, Don't start, and, Eat
your food, and one of us said, Fuck you, fucker, and our mother
said, Don't, and the mother said, Please keep eating, and one of us
started laughing, and our mother said, We're going now, and one
of us said in a scary voice, There were signs, and one of us spilled
the salt on the table, and one of us called for the dog who came
running over, and one of us threw the salt shaker at the dog, and
one of us beat our fists on the table, and one of us looked at our
mother and said, I'm in a mood, Lord, I'm in a mood, and one of
us started crying.

And on the way home from the dinner, in the back seat of
the wagon, one of us had a loose eyelash, and one of us said, Make
a wish, and one of us said, I wish I had twenty wishes, and one of
us said, You're crazy, and one of us said, You're the one crazy, and
one of us said, Fuck you, and one of us said, Fuck you, fucker, and
one of us said, Do you want to fight, and one of us said, I'll smack
you, and one of us said, I'll kick your ass, and one of us kicked the
other's ass, and our mother pulled onto the shoulder.

We rode the rest of the way home in silence. We pulled into
the drive. Our mother pushed the button. The garage door slowly
rose. She pulled the wagon into the garage. The coupe was there.

It had been there for weeks. Our mother said, Your father and his goddamn toys. She said, I'm going to hit it. We looked at each other. We thought about flicking our mother's neck for fun as she tried to park. She said, Watch me hit it. And we said, You won't hit it. And she said, Oh yes I will. She said, Watch me. Our mother pulled the wagon behind the coupe. She kept on going. She hit the coupe. She backed up. She hit it again.

Our father lifted his head from the steering wheel. He was not crying. He pulled the coupe onto the road and took us to get some ice cream. We ate our ice cream standing beside the coupe. The ground was made of loose dirt. We dug lines with our shoes into the ground. We kicked the dirt at each other's legs. We kicked the dirt at our father's legs. He kicked the dirt back and we laughed. Our ice cream was getting dirty, and we kicked the dirt high into the air. Our father kicked it hardest, and we were covered in dirt. Our ice cream was full of dirt. We were laughing. The dirt was flying everywhere, and we would like to say we laughed for a very long time.

It should have been a game of horse. It should have been our father home sick and a game of horse even with the air pump missing. Even with the basketball deflated in the weeds. Even with the sky looking like rain. It should have been a game, just us. The aim to score with the deflated ball. A shot with the eyes shut. Made. A shot with the eyes shut. Missed. An H. A one-handed shot. Made. A one-handed shot. Missed. An O. A shot from between the legs. Made. A shot from between the legs. Missed. An R. A two-handed shot. Made. A two-handed shot. Missed. An S. A shot from the walk. Made. A shot from the walk. Made. A shot from the walk. Made. A shot from the walk. Made. A shot from the walk. Made. A shot from the walk. Made. A shot from the walk. Made. A shot from the walk. Missed.

Court

There's me in my car and my car plays a song.

There's the ten over there on the court.

And the low sun going lower, the tall grass poking through cracks.

I watch the ten on the court do their circles, their footwork. How they orbit each other. How one is the sun, then another, another.

Five wear shirts and the others, well. I feel I shouldn't look. But I feel that also of the shirted ones. How their sweat shows skin below their shirts. How they stretch to the net and their underwear, their collarbones.

They go, Get on him, and, Fucker.

They scatter like sailors on a capsizing boat. They stand, hands frantic in the air.

Then they orbit one sun. Then they orbit another.

Everything juts when they jump to the hoop.

A shot.

It repeats.

It repeats.

And I'm in a rowboat floating in the deep.

I know it's not really a boat but a car.

I've never been stupid, despite what's been whispered.

My car is parked. It lurks in the flora. I call it flora. This growth through the cracks in the lot. And I lurk.

I watch through the windshield thinking, Hey there sailors, and of if I went, Sailors, of what that would mean to someone else. To some neighbor girl standing on her stoop.

The girls always go in each other's ears, Whisper whisper whisper.

I go, Take a picture, It'll last longer.

But there's no one in the flora but me. How it always is. Me in the flora, the boys on the court. Every evening in summer. In summers.

I find love songs on the radio. The ones that let thoughts become pictures.

I think of bare feet, wet grass. The clichéd crack of dawn.

I know dawn is not a crack but a smear.

Poetry turned it into a crack.

Poetry is why we have cliché.

It's for when science is too hard to grasp.

So there I am in the backyard in spring. I'm seventeen.

I try to imagine a boy, a blue shirt. He crosses my yard. He reaches for me.

But all I can see is my father's suitcase in the grass. My things are in it.

I'd run through grass until night.

But something inside my brain goes, Stay. Something inside goes, Graduate.

There's only a month left of school.

I go back inside before the sun reveals me.

I had dreamed of running though grass the whole way.

But there are eggs on the table. Two. Poached.

The eggs are cold.

My parents whisper in the other room. Their war has ended.

I wash my hands and eat the eggs.

Love songs speed at three four three meters per second.

In air that is. The speed of sound in air.

I learned this in high school. I also learned of the speed of light. One eight six thousand miles per second.

We're linked by speeding sound and light.

Thoughts I have on evenings like these. Thoughts of the type I often have.

I watch the clouds turn orange in the evenings. The tall stiff grass turns orange. This from sunlight. It strikes the flora and turns it to fire. Or to water. Depending on the time. Depending on where the sun is sitting.

And whatever the time and wherever the sun, I'm part of the flora. As is my car. As are the ten. We're linked.

This would perplex the neighbor girls. They think science is hard.

If they were smart they'd go, What about someone who's deaf and blind, What about him, How is he linked.

Meaning if he can't hear sound or see light. Yes, I get it.

Because, I'd go, The waves still touch him.

Sound waves, light waves are what I mean. The blind and deaf get touched by waves.

The girls would go, Stupid.

Though they're the ones stupid.

But if a tree falls in a forest, they'd go. If they were smart. I'd go, Cliché.

They've been trying to trip me up since high school.

They still stare when they stand on the stoops when I pass.

Take a picture girls, if you like.

All the neighbor girls have dropped out of college. All the neighbor girls are married with houses. They own their own stoops in the neighborhood. They own their own kids who stand on the stoops.

I think of one of the shirted ones in my car.

It goes like this: The ball sails over a shirted one's head. It rolls past my car. Into the flora. Toward the woods. The shirted one chases it down. He sees me sitting inside my car. I smoke a cigarette. I go, Hey there sailor. He goes, Give me a smoke. I go, Get in the car. He gets in the car.

The love song goes and goes.

Then one thing, another. We talk at first. The light leaves the car. We sit a bit closer. Then the song is what links us. Sound, that is. Then we link ourselves in other ways.

Touch, I'd go to the neighbor girls. To see them squirm.

I have spent whole nights in the flora. I have fallen asleep across the front seat.

At sunrise I've noticed the sky looks bruised.

I've been wanting to jot this down in the dust. I've been wanting to show this to one of the ten as he wakes by me on the seat.

But for now the sky's just turning orange. And they glow on the court while the low sun sits on their heads.

And if one of them goes, Take a picture, to me, I'll go, I look where I want.

Outside my brain I see skin beneath see-through white. I see them orbit each other on the court.

Inside my brain a finger slips up and up. The hair of a face on the hair of my face.

And regardless. Look. Inside my brain, we're fucking.

The neighbor girls would go, Why did she think that.

I'd go, Because I think.

The girls knew nothing in high school science. It was all I could do not to leave the classroom.

When they opened their mouths, I covered my ears and quietly sang.

They made their cracks. Their, What is she doing.

Even the teacher went, What in the world.

The girls all laughed.

The teacher went, Would you share your song.

When the ball bounces past to the woods, I duck. I duck when keys clink. Or when feet pound close.

I lower the song so they can't hear it.

And when they're back on the court, I turn it back up.

I never leave the car running in the flora.

I learned to play the radio with the car turned off. I learned to turn the car key backward. And the radio will play. And the lighter will work with the car turned off.

The pebbles on the car floor are rose quartz and white. The silver strips in the flora are mica.

I remember this from the last year of high school. And school ended one day after studying rocks.

The house was quiet for most of that summer.

Then a radio came by mail. My father's gift for ending high school. Mailed to the house near the end of summer. I kept it below the bed with the dust. It played love songs at night that let me have thoughts in pictures.

Thoughts of standing in the backyard grass.

I'm waiting for a boy to cross my yard. He's wearing blue.

And we run off together through the grass.

My father's suitcase is packed with my things.

I'd gone, Stop your fighting.

I'd gone, I'm leaving.

No one heard me as I packed.

I stood in the backyard waiting for him.

Of course, he knew nothing of this.

I went back in the house.

The sun rose.

I ate.

When I leave in the evenings my mother watches from the window. I can see her face pressed to the glass.

She's jealous.

My car seat is softer than hers ever was.

Soft enough to sleep on. And so on.

My radio worked for weeks before it didn't.

It was a whole life change when the radio stopped. I lay in the dark below my bed. Blind and deaf with the radio off. I could feel my arms fuzzed in the dust.

I wrote to my father for the first time ever. I found his address in my mother's drawer.

I wrote, The radio broke, on the back of a scrap. I mailed it to him.

He sent a used car in place of the radio. It was left in the drive behind my mother's.

I don't know who drove it and left it.

High school ended years ago. Was it seven years. It was maybe eight. Regardless.

I recall it ended with science. And science ended with rocks. I learned to tell quartz in a rock pile. Big deal.

And the science teacher wore a shade of blue. And his eyes. I could tell but won't.

He went, Perhaps this could be your major in college.

And he meant it.

The dust on the dash takes my handprint and keeps it.

I stop when I find a love song.

It looks like they're dancing to the song, the ten.

They go, Mother, and, Fucker. They grunt in ways like in war. They slap five.

Give me some skin, we once went on the stoops.

Give me some skin, and we slid our palms as kids.

I'm happiest when the ball whooshes through without touching the rim.

Just imagine fucking that way.

I can hear the neighbor girls go, Why did she say that.

But imagine a clean whoosh whoosh whoosh.

I often think to join their game. I'd stand on the court in a high school pose. Sunshined hair flipped to one side of my neck. Head slightly tilted, wind whipping my skirt. And I'd ask for a light. I'd ask for a ride.

But the car, the neighbor girls would go. If they were smart.

What about her car, Why would she need a ride, they'd go. There's her car parked in the flora.

Good questions.

Plus the car lighter. They'd be perplexed. Why would she need a light, they'd go.

I'd twirl my hair. I'd go, Okay, boys, The car's mine, You caught me. But the lighter's broken, I'd also go.

How my mother's car lighter pushed in, stayed in. I know it's possible to break a car lighter.

I know it's possible to break a whole car. Look at my mother's. Four flat tires. Doors stuck open. Broken windows. And inside are years of weather. Inside are rough torn seats and broken switches and the lighter that never popped out.

Though the horn still blares. She always yells when I blare it. I never really do it now except to test it.

My mother's always pounding head.

Her shut off car makes ticking sounds.

Her dark kitchen which I stay from.

A card on my car went, Happy sixteen.

Though I was seventeen, almost eighteen.

Should anyone ask: I'm doing a study on ball, Taking notes on boys, For a college paper for when I go to college.

They go, Motherfucker! And, Inside!

Their rib cages jut with each shot.

I see underwear when they raise their arms.

But I'm not going to college yet.

I just want away from the quiet house.

And the twilight reminds me of an old shirt.

Not of a certain shirt but a certain color.

The science teacher. He wore this color. He meant nothing to me. He's a blur.

My mother still keeps the house clean.

There are places to sit in the kitchen by windows.

When I leave the house I go, I'm going to study, and big deal when I walk in after dark. It's only my mother in her shut off kitchen. I'm sitting on the stoop, I lie and who cares.

Big deal when I walk in the next morning after sleeping the night alone in the car.

I was out with the girls.

My mother silent in her kitchen.

The keys were left inside the car.

I started the car and drove.

School was starting back up again.

The boys were playing five-on-five.

My mother found me in the dark in her car. She held my arms and dragged me.

This was high school. Broken windows. A drag through grass. A door slam. A door slam. Another.

A wonder I could keep my head up high.

But the radio came at the end of summer. The radio saved my brain.

The neighbor girls all went, She's crazy, Keep away.

The neighbor girls made plans for their lives back then. Engagements. Showers. Kids.

When we meet by mistake on the stoops nowadays: So what are you doing with yourself. So what are you doing. I asked you first.

And so on and so on.

A wonder I can keep my head on straight.

And should I go, I'm sitting in the car. Should I go, I'm watching five-on-five with songs in my car. Trust me, they'd think the same old thing.

That I stole rocks from science.

That I fucked the teacher.

That I never could mix.

Sometimes there are nine. They play half-court four-on-four and the odd one shoots alone.

I consider a game with the odd one. A game of one-on-one.

And so what if he beats me. I'm no teen and it's not about winning. It's about contact. It's about sitting in the car afterward.

You know how it happens.

One thing, another. I look at his mouth. He looks at my eyes looking at his mouth. I look at his eyes looking at my eyes.

And so on.

I sat in my mother's car with the rocks on the dash. Fool's gold. Mica. Quartz. Like pulled-up treasures from a capsized boat. I made wave shapes in the dust on the dash with my fingers. For a sense of sand, of wet.

I was captain of a boat. I had stopped on the shore to look at my treasures.

I knew I was not in a boat but a car.

This is metaphor. Poetry.

Because the science of this was too hard. I admit it.

Because the science of this was not of rocks. I understood rocks.

The science of this was of the brain.

I took the rocks from the classroom when the teacher was gone. I put them in my pockets.

I cannot describe how they looked on the dash with the sun coming through.

Then it got dark.

I blared the horn until dragged to the house.

The neighbors came out to their stoops.

The neighbor girls went, Did you hear what she did.

They went, She's crazy.

Well, there's no fighting in the house nowadays.

World War Three, the neighbor girls called it.

They went, World War Three down at her house.

They tried to trip me when I passed.

The cliché goes, You'll go blind.

And once I almost did. I was in the car and love songs played. So thoughts took over. My face pressed to a shirted one's shirt. The shirt is blue. My face pressed so tight it feels like drowning. Like drowning in the ocean. Or in the sky. Or some other poetic bullshit cliché. A clichéd drowning in my brain. A clichéd fucking and fucking and fucking.

I stopped when I could. I had blindness sorting back to vision.

I saw the ten again as ten on the court.

For weeks it was me and the radio.

I hid beneath my bed singing radio songs. I made pictures from thoughts.

Me, the suitcase. The boy in blue. And this time we run through the grass.

But the boy in the blue shirt was never a boy. And he was never going anywhere I was.

And I was singing too loud at night went my mother.

She went, Do you know what it is to feel a pounding from inside.

She went, Do you know what it is to hear a pounding like a drum.

She went, Inside your brain.

I sat in my mother's car with twilight coming blue through the quartz. They were fighting inside. Then it got dark. There was no more light coming through.

They thought I couldn't hear the fight. But I heard it clear. At three four three.

My father went, Crazy.

My mother went, Crazy.

They thought I couldn't see the fight. But I saw his hand flash through the air.

So I took the rocks to the car.

The neighbor girls could hear the war from their stoops.

I could still hear it clear.

I blared the horn to drown it out.

I was captain of my boat. I was thinking of my treasures.

Everyone heard the car horn blaring. Every dumb girl from every damn stoop.

My mother and father came running outside. My mother pressed her face to the window. I wouldn't get out of the car. I had locked the doors. The windows were up. I couldn't hear my mother screaming.

She smashed the windows to get me out. What did she use. A rock, I suppose. A rock from the drive. From the weeds.

No. It wasn't a rock. It was a clump of cement. Conglomerate, we called it in high school science. A mix of rocks.

She didn't have to smash all the windows in.

I was sinking it felt like before she smashed.

My mother dragged me into the house. There were cuts to clean.

My father took his suitcase. He took his car.

My car hides in the tall blue grass. My soft-seated car from my father.

There are no windows to my mother's car. All crashed-in holes. There's no use hiding in that car.

The neighbor girls went, What is she thinking.

Thoughts, I thought and left it at that.

I returned the rocks to the classroom. I finished high school.

No hard feelings.

The teacher let it slide.

He thought I was going to college.

The neighbor girls went, Keep away from her if you know what's good.

When I sang in class that day, I felt the spotlight. Everyone laughed.

When the radio came in the mail with a card I thought, If only sooner.

If only I had known the radio songs to sing in class.

What was it I sang in there.

Row Row Row Your Boat.

The girls all laughed.

My face got hot.

The neighbor girls go, Whisper whisper.

Their hands flash out.

Their kids duck on the stoops.

The radio card went, Congratulations.

I had graduated And no hard feelings.

I played the radio until my mother took it away.

Later that night I went, Where is it.

My mother wouldn't let on. She just laughed into a cry.

I was screaming from the stoop, Where the fuck is it.

The neighbor girls went, Still crazy.

I found it smashed in the weeds by my mother's car. I stooped to the weeds and picked up the pieces. Some were very small and some were from the insides.

I'd never blare my horn. The ten would hear it blaring.

They'd turn to see me ducking to the floor.

They'd come up to the window. They'd ask what I was doing.

I'd step out of the car.

I'd go, Hey there sailors, I'm looking for my cigarette, It fell to the floor, Do you have a cigarette.

Or, Hey sweeties, Have you boys seen my boyfriend, He's this tall and he comes here to play one-on-one, He wears a blue shirt.

Or, Hey you sailor-boys, Do you go to this high school, I went to this high school, I'm doing a study on ball.

Or, Hey darlings, Do you know how to change a fuse, I think my fuse has blown.

I saw his hand flash through the air. I saw it reach her face.

I didn't care that his hand flashed through the air. I didn't care that she didn't duck.

I didn't care that he left and never came back.

I cared that he left me with her.

Once I was seventeen.

I stood in the grass before the sun rose.

The grass felt wet beneath my feet.

Then the sun began.

Then everything tried to grow.

If the ball bounces past I'll jump out to chase it. I'll pretend to take it. I'll go, Just kidding, boys, and toss the ball.

If it travels to the woods' edge I'll chase it and stop it and toss it at the speed of sound. Three four three. In air that is.

I'll toss it in a blink to the boys going how the girls once went on the stoops throwing rocks, Think quick!

And if they laugh going, What's think quick, like it's some kind of way we spoke way back but don't speak now, I'll laugh too. I mean I'm no teen striking a pose. I know these boys won't give me some skin. I've never been stupid despite what they think. I know these boys won't fuck me.

There was a time that they'd have fucked me.

But back then I never fucked.

Back then I only wanted one.

He had eyes like blue topaz.

I said I wouldn't say it. But it has to sound poetic. It's a harder science than light and waves.

He had a shirt the same color as his eyes.

I admit like twilight through quartz.

Soon the ten will all be shirted. They'll slap five and walk off the court.

I'll be tempted to shine my lights on them. To blare the horn. To go, through the window, Hey.

He went, Good job, when I spotted fool's gold in the rock pile on the table in the classroom.

The girls went, Crazy motherfucker, when they found the rocks in my locker. And they found what they called my poems.

But they weren't really poems. I wasn't some bullshit poet.

They were notes on rocks. On the teacher's shirt.

They called them poems.

They called them love notes.
But I called it science.

I went to my mother, I'm going to college.
My mother went, You're going nowhere.
My father went, I'm going now.
I mean to say my father went. And I went, Wait.

Soon the ten will walk to my car. They'll pass the ball back
and forth.
I'll be tempted to turn the radio up. To step out from the car
and go, Hey boys.
But they'll walk fast though the flora, and I'll lower the song
and duck to the floor as they pass.

Once I was seventeen. I had thoughts of being eighteen.
Now I'm this. I have thoughts of seventeen.

Once the girls went, You're really crazy.
And I went, Better crazy than stupid.

Once the girls went, How's it going.
And I went, It's going, and left it at that.

Once the girls went, Give me some skin.
And we slid our palms like any kids.

Static

knowing the good of sunstreaked hair, of toothpick legs, a sweet ass hula-shaking on the boardwalk, a soft sweet ass shaking into the boys, hair teased into waves, toothpick legs and pointed tits and big hands on those perfect tits, bear paws squeezing like they're squeezing peaches, like they're squeezing overripe tomatoes, how overripe anything squashes when squeezed, how his bleach-blonde girlfriend's squash when your father squeezes in the kitchen of the beach house when you're standing in the doorway, when you shouldn't be, watching,

knowing to push your tits into the boy you like, to press them into his chest where he stands by the House of Mirrors when you walk on the boardwalk with the local girls, your boy's hands in his pockets to shift his hard-on, all the girls going how hot he is, how hard his dick is, going you can tell by the way he's standing, slouched, that he's got a hard-on, going, I'd only throw him out of bed to fuck him on the floor, going, Look at his mouth when he looks at you, and, Mouth *orange juice* at him when he looks at you, because it looks sexy to mouth the words *orange* and *juice*, like you're going something else, like you're going, Aren't you sexy, the way your lips go around the words like that,

knowing to eat your cotton candy slow as you can, to tongue it slow off the paper cone, and to wear shades of blue so later he'll see the ocean and sky and the blue lights blinking on the Flying Bobs and he'll remember you wore no shoes,

feet deep in sand in the days, the air so hot you can't see the tip of your cigarette smolder, watching kites in the sky like birds through slit eyes, half dozing on a beach towel, half thinking how maybe tonight you'll let your boy press his mouth to yours and hard, you'll let him put his hands on your ass and squeeze if he wants, as you don't want to come off as some kind of cocktease like your father's trying-to-be-grown-up girlfriend who pushes your father when he tries to get her going in the beach house kitchen, her toothpick legs beginning to buckle, all that pawing and kissing when you shouldn't be watching, but there you are hoping to see something, fucking,

your ass a peach, a ripe tomato, your boy could reach out and squeeze, and you can bet he loves peaches, though not tomatoes, how your father hates how they squash and the seeds and the mess of all that juice when the girlfriend cuts tomatoes on the kitchen counter and the tomatoes squirt like what, Like a pussy, your fat uncle poking a fork into an uncut tomato on the kitchen counter, Like a virgin's pussy, when the tomato squirts red, your father going to your fat uncle, Shut your fat face, your fat uncle laughing, his face turning purple and splotched, uglier than a face should be,

knowing the good of sunstreaked hair teased into waves, eyes shadowed shimmery up to the brows, his hands all over your face, your tits, the two of you dug into a rut in the night-cold sand in the cave below the boardwalk well after the tourists leave for their hotels, well after the boardwalk shuts down for the night, and the seagulls picking at paper and bottle caps above your heads, and the waves far out and crashing in a way that makes you think of a million dishes crashing to a kitchen floor, and the trashpicker who pokes at trash with a stick and sings in the mornings when the beach is empty, and the sand on your boy, on his suntanned skin, and that coconut smell, that dirt sweat smell that makes you think, for a second, that your life is a life,

a yellow silk nightgown hanging on a hook on the back of the washroom door, your father's girlfriend's nightgown you've never seen her wear but have looked at on the hook in the washroom on nights you're getting ready to meet the kids on the boardwalk, making your face shimmer silver above the eyes, blue below, red on the lips, the ruffles around the neck of the nightgown like daisy petals on overgrown daisies,

knowing you're hot as any local girl, squeezing juice on your head to lighten your hair, untying your top to tan your back, always shoeless because who the fuck cares about splinters from the boardwalk, and who the fuck cares about cigarette butts pressed to your feet or the heat of the sand if you walk on the sand, dynamite making his dick hard like that, making it push beneath his pants pocket like you have some magic force that can turn things to stone just by hula-shaking nights with the local girls, just by smoking on the boardwalk, pushing your smoke out in the pucker you practice in the washroom mirror, a pucker learned from TV nurses and waitresses and girl cops dressed in tight tan pants, and those TV teachers, their walk to the chalkboard, their pants creeping up their cracks, your father going from his place on his chair back home, one hand tucked beneath his waistband, Will you look at that, and, Do you think she's a sexpot, so you'll go, No, so he'll laugh at you, going, Better than you, going, She's a peach, and, Your face could freeze time,

mouthing the words *orange* and *juice*, the boys all going, Come here with that, the boys all going, Come here C. S. L., for cock sucking lips, going, Bring that pussy over here,

your father, your fat uncle drinking beers on the sun porch, your uncle going, Where's the little girl, your father going, She's in the john, going, She's in a mood, how he does about the girlfriend when she swats him away with the back of her hand when you're caught watching touching when you shouldn't be watching, when she's a soft peach getting softer in his paws and she ducks out from his grip, your father going, What, the girlfriend going, Not now, your father going, You're in a mood,

never knowing how to talk to boys, never knowing how to talk to grown-ups, not wanting to talk to your father's girlfriends at the beach, every summer a new bleach-blonde with toothpick legs and pointed tits and a boardwalk night shift, funnel cake maker, ride operator, souvenir seller, never able to order your own food in the boardwalk diners, the grown-ups going to the sunburned waiters,

She'll have fried eggs, She'll have buttered toast, She'll have grape jelly, burnt bacon, because they know what you need, they know how you like it, and you never speak up when you should be speaking, thinking what if you fuck up and they laugh at you in front of a waiter and what if he's hot and you cry at the table and they laugh even harder and it never ends,

dynamite getting yourself off face down in the sand by rolling slightly against the sand, by pressing slightly, thinking thoughts of your boy behind the House of Mirrors, thinking of him and you below the boardwalk making out hard in the night-cold sand, your boy's hands squeezing your ass, your tits, your boy's hands squeezing your father's girlfriend's tits, your father squeezing the girlfriend's tits, your father's paws going down her pants, the girlfriend undoing your father's buckle, your boy,

your father and your fat uncle smoking on the sun porch, your father's girlfriend working night shift on the boardwalk, and you in the washroom putting on the girlfriend's makeup, more than your usual, made up like a sexpot like the TV sexpots, teasing your hair into something big, trying on the nightgown to see if it fits, finding it fits a bit large in places, long in others, but overall close, swiveling your hips in the girlfriend's nightgown in the washroom mirror in the figure eight you learned from TV when your father was sleeping in his chair in the room back home and the show switched to something, the news, then something, some late night show and instructions on how to hula dance, the host of the show in some awkward swivel, painful to watch, and the audience laughing and clapping as you tried out the swivel in front of the TV until your father waked in a snap with a sudden, Don't, and went back to sleep, your father and your fat ugly uncle looking as you slowly walk across the sun porch, the sun porch already a haze of smoke, as you sit on a chair in the girlfriend's nightgown, as you spread your legs some then snap them shut before anyone sees, crossing your legs at the ankles and going, What,

knowing the good of eyes like smoke, like smoldering ash, the brown eyes you line with blue, the brown hair you streak with lemon juice, your white bra padded enough to have something soft and big to press into your boy's chest, going, Look but don't touch, behind the House of Mirrors, going, Glad you thought about it though, Glad you noticed, Thanks for looking, Look again sometime, walking past with the girls and laughing by the Flying Bobs, laughing when the boys call you C. S. L., when they call you cocktease,

appearing behind the House of Mirrors the first night at the beach after your father goes, Don't get back too late, and appearing, shoe-less, in from the city, What's your name, Susan, Where you from, The city, What city, Baltimore, the local kids knowing you're hard as coconut, hard as stone, this tourist from the city who knows this beach is some stupid crazy land of spinning kites and every damn ride on the boardwalk spinning, the Himalayan, the Flying Bobs, songs playing up so loud on those rides every tourist in every hotel can hear them playing nights, the local boys going, Sweet Susie Q, the local girls going, Don't listen to them, the man at the Flying Bobs going, Do you want to go faster, the kids on the ride going, Yes, the songs so loud they get stuck in your head the way pictures get stuck in your head,

someone on the sun porch seeing, your fat uncle seeing, a quick glimpse of something, you can tell, as he raises his eyebrows and looks at your father, wanting to be invisible from some magic force that can turn you to cloud when you have to turn to cloud so your father can't see you come in at sunrise, so the girlfriend can't see you with the kids on the boardwalk, so she can't see you picking at your salad at the table and go, Eat your salad, pretending she's a grown-up when she's closer to your age than to your father's, a local your father met on the beach, her top untied to tan her back,

going, Give me a smoke, to some local girl who smells like sweat, who wears her hair the way you wear yours, long, streaked, who dresses how you dress, Give me a smoke, before walking past your boy, your boy going, Come here Susie Q, Where you going Susie Q, Where you going sexy girl, and you going, I don't know where I'm going, and, Why should I, making the local girls laugh,

not eating your eggs and bacon in the diner, not looking up at the sunburned waiter, your head full of blue lights, blinking lights, thinking of your boy and what you'll do tonight, what you'll let him do,

your father going he's been spending too much time with the girlfriend and he's got nothing to do before your fat uncle comes over tonight for beers and he'd like to take you to the boardwalk for a good dinner and a ride on the Ferris wheel, Father daughter, Won't that be fun, going you've been running around the boardwalk nights like some kind of crazy local, the girlfriend has seen you, has seen the crowd of kids clustered on the boardwalk, going, Wouldn't a night together be fun, just you two on the Ferris wheel, cotton candy, Father daughter, Dinner first,

crazy when you don't let your boy grab your arm, the boys all going, Cocktease, going, Suck my dick, laughing, doubled over, the

local girls laughing, a crazy spinning in your gut going faster faster, then faster when you let your boy touch your arm, when you let him grab hold of your arm, the girls all laughing, the girls all going, Look at you, your boy all looking at your face and you let him look, you let him lean in as if to kiss your lips, your father's girlfriend rushing past the House of Mirrors to get to work, your father's girlfriend pretending not to see you, but she sees you, you know, and she ignores you, the girlfriend walking faster, your boy going, Cocktease, when you wriggle away,

your father ordering you fried clams, fried potatoes, your father drinking a beer and going, Let's ride the Ferris wheel, trying to look excited, like the Ferris wheel is any big thing,

the girlfriend looking at the black bottoms of your feet when your feet are on up the kitchen table when she's chopping tomatoes, like she has any right looking at your feet, like she has any right going, when your father leaves the kitchen, I saw you last night,

your father calling you old maid because you can't decide on pink or blue and it's just cotton candy for fuck's sake, and really you don't want cotton candy, but your father wants to buy you one, and who can't decide on cotton candy when it all tastes the same, your father going, Old maid, when you can't decide so it's pink you decide on, your father going, Girlie, when you decide on pink,

thinking, as the waves crash to bits, as the kites make their crazy loops, how tonight you'll let him kiss you if he wants,

the girlfriend going, I saw you last night, going, I saw you with those kids, going, Is that boy your boyfriend, I won't tell your father, you going, Shut your fat face,

Baltimore, that nothing place of outside smokestacks, gray sky, brick, and inside TV, hula dancers, sand and blue, TV static, your father asleep in his chair,

seen on TV, some who knows what show, some show for teens, some teenage girl going, Boys like girls in light blue,

always a cocktease, always wriggling,

in line, your father holding your ticket and your hand, going, The boys over there are looking at you, pointing to behind the House of Mirrors where the kids are already standing, smoking, even though it's still light, even though things don't happen until after dark, the songs already up loud on the rides, the songs that stick in your head, and the songs will stay stuck in your head for long, for how long, for as long as you live, and you'll hear them in cars and stores and streets when you're a grown-up dragging your ass through a space and you'll want to cry because everything has changed and nothing has changed,

your father going, Who are those boys, like some kind of boy-friend, like some kind of jealous fucking boyfriend, your father going, You're a funny girl, when your face gets hot, going, Funny looking, Ha ha, A face that could stop a clock,

the girlfriend turning soft in your father's paws, your father reaching inside her pants, your boy's hands inside her pants, your boy's hands inside your pants, the kites soaring faster than birds,

your father going, Are those your friends, those boys, and, Do you know them, and, What about those girls, and, They're looking at you, pointing to the local kids who point back from where they stand behind the House of Mirrors smoking cigarettes, laughing at you, some of them waving, some of them calling out things to you like, Daddy's girl, like, Hi Daddy, like, Hi C. S. L., your father shaking his head at them, your father looking at the local girls, looking at their asses like peaches, their dynamite asses, your father looking at the way they hula-shake them into the boys to the music coming from the Flying Bobs, your father going, Will you look at that, your father calling them the local sexpots, his bear paw sweating around your hand, What are you doing with the local sexpots,

pushing slightly into the hard hot sand thinking, Do you want to go faster, Yes, Do you want to go faster, God, yes, God, no,

the man at the Ferris wheel going, No shoes no ride, your father pulling you out of line, the two of you walking to a souvenir shop to buy too-big shoes, plastic shoes, Maryland written across the sides in red,

the girlfriend chopping tomatoes faster, you going, You saw nothing last night, standing up from the table and pushing the girlfriend's pile of chopped tomatoes to the floor,

a short trip on the Ferris wheel, your father screaming, your gut caught in your throat,

the boys going, Cocktease, like you don't know this, like you don't know what you are,

knowing you can't go back to the boardwalk, not tonight, not ever, knowing the local kids will have something to go, this hard as coconut city girl, you, this stupid little girl, you, this stupid little fuck letting your father hold your hand in line because you couldn't go no, because you couldn't make yourself invisible, you couldn't turn yourself to cloud, you couldn't freeze time by stopping all the clocks with your face as ugly and splotched as a face can be, because you have no magic force, letting your father go, Wheee, when the Ferris wheel brought you down and down, the kids all calling out, Daddy's girl,

walking a quick walk back to the beach house, a block ahead of your father, walking into the beach house alone, slamming and locking the washroom door, staring at yourself in the washroom mirror, putting on the girlfriend's makeup and heavy, like a fucking sexpot, teasing the hair into some big thing,

sitting on the sun porch thinking, I'm sitting on a chair, The men are looking, The men are looking at me, The men are looking at me sitting on a chair, My life is over, My life was nothing, But I could get up,

tiptoeing into the beach house at sunrise, your father asleep in a chair, your father waking and going, What, and falling back to sleep,

and it could have been good with your boy below the boardwalk, his hands caught up in your sunstreaked hair,

it could have been good had you meant it, had you not been such a cocktease, always wriggling, then wriggling away,

your fat ugly uncle looking at you how he looks at your father's girlfriend, his mouth forming a whistle you never hear because there's no whistle but your fat uncle going, Sexy, and the girlfriend turns red, Sexy, and you run back to the washroom, screaming, Shut the fuck up, your fat uncle still calling, Come out sexy, your father going, Shut your fat face, your fat uncle still laughing his head off, your head a shadow in the corner, your hair a mess after all that teasing,

knowing it's over, the boardwalk, the beach, knowing you'll go back home, Baltimore, back to school, brick, smoke, gray, that nothing life of TV, you on the couch, your father sleeping on his chair, TV static, clear gloss on your lips,

knowing you'll still hear your fat uncle going, Sexy, in your head, like seeing a picture in your head, like seeing TV in your head, when you're a grown-up dragging your sorry ass through your house,

sitting on the washroom floor in the girlfriend's nightgown, the girlfriend's makeup, and you didn't mean to be so sexy in the nightgown, sitting in the corner when you've gone too far, and you didn't mean to be so sexy,

your father knocking on the washroom door, going, Come out now, going, Wipe that shit off your face, going, Put on some clothes and act like a grown-up, going, Walking around in that crazy getup, Where'd you get such a crazy getup,

your father's girlfriend rushing past the House of Mirrors when the boardwalk shuts down for the night, the local kids walking home from the boardwalk, you walking down to the beach,

your head like TV, pictures shifting, a switch and switch and switch, and it could have been good in the cave below the boardwalk with your boy, but you're what, you're a cocktease, and there's no deep rut you dug below the boardwalk with your boy,

your head like TV, late night static, something forbidden behind the snow,

your father kicking open the door,

your father going, Come out, from his place in the doorway, his shadow filling the corner,

you going, Come here, from your place in the corner, your father not coming closer,

and it could have been good with your boy below the boardwalk, his hands caught up in your sunstreaked hair,

instead of you alone in the night-cold sand watching the waves until sunrise,

the trashpicker poking at trash with a stick, singing, Susie Q, Oh Susie Q,

you running heavy on the still cold sand,

you running breathless into light blue light,

the Ferris wheel small in the distance, static,

How It Starts

This will be about several things—no surprise, what isn't.

But I'll start with a convention I went to each year.

This, despite my brother's words, my mother's, despite it all. For we all know of conventions and the ones who, each year, go.

Let me say this. I wasn't one of those ones, you know. You couldn't call me a die-hard goer. I mean I went to this convention yearly, yes. But I know I could have lived without it. I wasn't one of those desperate die-hards, living for the day we all convened.

My brother—let's face it—was jealous. He had no conventions to call his own. He had hobbies, however, as a kid. Model airplanes, butterflies stuck with pins.

He caught the butterflies with his hands in the field behind our house. There was nothing much in the field. Wildflowers and tall brown grass.

There was a way he stood, bent and low, his hands an inverted cup.

He dropped the butterflies into a plastic bag. He sprayed something into the bag to make the butterflies stop flapping their wings. Then he tied the bag at the top.

From the field we could see the back of our house.

And the terror of this perspective.

My father went to conventions. Medical ones. Though he was not in the medical field. But he liked to meet people who were. Like, for example, nurses. Or those women who longed to be nurses.

When we were kids, my father said to me and my brother to choose a convention, any one, when we were grown. He said, It gets you out of the office.

So I, grown, chose a convention which seemed fitting at the time, its topic that is, which I won't divulge except to say it's in the field, though I am not, of showbiz. I saw the convention mentioned in the back of a magazine, and it looked to me to have potential, far more than my father's, which were often dull in dull hotels, men at tables in the saddest suits.

And they never gave us anything good. Tongue depressors with company names printed on them in red.

My mother, brother, and I spent evenings watching TV in the room. My brother built his model airplanes on the floor.

The room smelled of glue and paint. The fumes did something to my head.

My mother would say, without looking from the TV, Cap that glue.

My father went to cocktail lounges with friends from the convention. My mother waited up, ready to fight when he walked in late. My brother and I pretended to sleep.

My father would say, Can you let it go. He smelled of things. Sometimes we heard a crash.

We spent days at the beach if there was a beach. In rain we spent days in the room.

And now I associate hotel rooms with rain.

Which is to say the brochure arrived for the convention hotel—it arrived at the office—and I thought of rain.

The girls from the office looked over my shoulders. I pointed out the size of the hotel beds. They were very big, made for two, at least.

I pointed out, too, the indoor pool, the cocktail lounge.

The girls from the office, jealous I think, said, What a nice pool.

And there was the ballroom, the chandelier. I could see how the tables would get set up. I could see myself walking the ballroom at dusk, collecting things from the tables.

This year I would wear high-heeled shoes.

The girls from the office said, Why not swim.

Funny to be thinking of swimming. It was winter.

And I didn't even own a swimsuit.

Once, though, I did—it was two piece, blue—and once I could swim like a fish. I dove into waves and outswam my brother. He tried to outswim me but never could.

God I could tell you how he cried on the sand when a wave knocked him down to his knees.

In the room, later, I'd call him a baby and he'd catch me and pin me to the floor.

He'd whisper into my ear, You're dead.

I walked the ballroom in an evening dress and high-heeled shoes. I stopped at tables to have a look at the things the men were giving away. Pens, pencils. Handfuls of candies. The occasional tote bag.

I'd give the things to the girls from the office. They would fight for the tote bags. It was always this.

And I'll say right now—why waste time—that this year's convention was awful.

I blame, in part, a nonevent—I can say that now—which seemed an event as I, poolside, watched the men in the pool.

So I called my shrink from the room.

The operator said, What's your name, and I waited at first but then gave my name as one has to do this for collect.

The operator said, Well, how about that.

She said, My daughter has your same name.

And yes, I know—time has passed—how foolish it was to call my shrink collect.

On the first day, my shrink had said, Tell me about your father.

I said, He works in an office, and so on.

She said, Tell me about your mother.

My mother was dead, and my father had a girlfriend.

He said, I have a right to have a girlfriend.

My shrink said, How do you feel about that.

I thought up some jokes. How did I feel.

Well, I said, With my hands, of course.

When we went with my father to his conventions, I often ran up the hotel room bills. I called girls I knew from junior high when there was nothing else to do in the days. I knew many girls, though none of them well, and called despite how they likely felt about me.

My father pointed to the bills when checking out and said, You should have called collect.

He said, You'll send us to the poorhouse.

I sometimes imagined the poorhouse as a shack on the edge of some great road.

I talked with men in the ballroom before it turned dark. I laughed at their jokes.

So a man walks into a bar...

So a one-armed man...

A one-winged bird...

A horse and a nun walk into a bar and the horse says...

They loved to bend my ear.

It was so overwhelming. All those men. Their pathetic suits.

All those jokes to work through.

So a lady's car breaks down on the road, and she's walking along the roadside, and she sees a house with the light on—it's night—and when she gets to the house, she sees a man in the stable grooming the horses, and she walks up to the man and says, Mister, I'm wondering if you can help...

I looked into their eyes assertively. Longingly.

They were never looking at my eyes.

And I often laughed before the punch line. It was something

with timing. Something with their timing. It was always off. Or was it too on. There was often this pause before the punch line. And I often laughed in the pause.

Well, I knew about jokes. I was one to make them when I could.

Even when shopping for the swimsuit, I thought up a joke or two to tell.

The salesgirl had said, Can I help.

And I thought up jokes. I mean could she help. Of course she could. But not in the ways she thought.

I mean she could have helped me to be more assertive for one. Better looking for another.

She followed me from rack to rack.

She said, Are you going to the beach.

I said, No, a convention.

She said, Oh, what for.

But I couldn't come up with anything good. So I chose a swimsuit from the rack and parted the fitting room curtain. The suit fit tight in places—I'll just say it—tight all over.

The salesgirl called from the other side, Let's see you.

I pushed aside the curtain. She looked and said, Look at you.

She said, Well, you'll certainly turn heads in that.

And I almost made another joke. I almost said, Which way do you think the heads will turn.

Okay. But I didn't say it.

There were times to keep quiet and I knew these times.

The operator said her daughter had my name, and what was I supposed to say. She said something about how she chose her daughter's name because it meant something else, the name, something beautiful in some other language. And she said something about names in general and something about my mother choosing the same name and then the joke about great minds thinking alike and so on, as if she were the one with a foot in the door of something showbiz.

There was an evening at home I called my shrink. She picked up quick, a fluke, that time, as she, too, was trying to make a call.

I felt awful that evening, desperate, frantic, sitting on the floor, rocking back and forth, clutching my new swimsuit to my chest.

I couldn't tell if she was disappointed to find me on the other end.

But we talked for a moment. About what. About my body. My body inside a cagelike swimsuit. And the salesgirl had looked. And the men would look. And how was I supposed to wear the swimsuit in front of the men in the indoor pool when the suit didn't even fit.

The salesgirl had suggested I buy a terrycloth beachrobe as well. And I felt awful, in part, because of this. I felt awful, in part, because I thought she thought I should cover the ill-fitting swimsuit. And I felt awful, in part, because I had never before owned a beachrobe, as I always thought beachrobes for older women, like women old as my mother was when we traveled, who, at the beach, sat beneath a huge umbrella in her terrycloth beachrobe, shivering, who knew why.

Because she was sick.

Yes.

We didn't know it yet.

But we should have known it by the way she stared, unblinking, at the TV.

And her face was gray.

She slept like the dead.

My beachrobe, like hers, was short and white.

God, no one prepares one for anything.

The operator told me her daughter played several sports in high school, three sports, who knows which.

She said her daughter would someday be a professional something or other.

Had I been more assertive, I would have said, I don't care about your daughter. I would have said, Your daughter sounds like the bitches I knew in junior high.

Those girls ganged up on me for reasons I can't explain.

And did I play sports in high school, the operator wanted to know.

No, I did not. I played no sports in high school.

But I could swim like a fish my mother said.

Often there was no beach or it was fall or winter or about to rain and my mother and brother would go to a nearby mall to buy model airplanes and the glue my brother used that sent my head through the roof.

On those days, I watched TV in the room and called the girls from back home. If one didn't pick up, I called another, often one I hardly knew. I called as many girls as I could think of until I got through to one and then kept her on the phone for as long as

I could, just talking about unimportant things, even when she said
she had to go, her mother was calling her name.

What a sick feeling in my gut when we disconnected.

I had thoughts of, Who next, Who next, Who next.

And that dial tone, that terror sound from space.

The pool was filled with treading men, their heads bobbing
in the deep end.

I stood poolside, half-in half-out of the beachrobe.

This shouldn't have been so intense.

But look. Once I was a girl.

And my father and brother fell to their knees, rolled to their
backs.

My mother said from her place on the sand, Quit carrying
on.

My father said, Would you look at that.

He said, You can't even pinch an inch.

Well, I was no longer that thin, for what that's worth. I saw
that in the dressing room mirror. There was certainly more than
an inch.

My father looked at my legs and laughed. My legs were like
boys' legs then.

Well, I no longer had boys' legs for what that's worth.

My father said, Don't cry.

And I never knew which way to run. Either into the ocean or
into the room. It depended on which way my brother might run.
And it depended on the sky.

To make me laugh my father said, What's black and white
and red all over.

I never laughed.

My brother said, What.

The operator said, Are you calling a friend.

And I said, Yes.

A good friend, I said.

The operator's daughter had good friends too. They all played sports and why was it, she wanted to know, I didn't play sports.

I just didn't want to. I was always traveling with my family.

Oh, travel is good too. Did you go to Europe.

No, we went to Detroit and Miami and Tuscaloosa.

The operator said, Sports keep you in shape.

I almost joked, In the shape of what.

The operator said, My daughter has a figure, I used to have a figure.

And as I waited for the phone to ring, I wanted connection already. I wanted that feeling of seeing a face, a familiar face one wants to see.

Like one's mother's face, to take this further. One's mother's face in a crowd.

But you get old, you know, the operator said, and the figure goes, Ha, I used to eat whatever I wanted, My daughter eats like a horse and never gains, And the boys, You should see the boys around her, I never had boys...

And as the phone started ringing, I considered saying that my friend wasn't home, that I'd try again later when she was sure to be home and waiting for my call.

I wasn't feeling right about calling my shrink collect.

I had not been back to see my shrink for weeks, and I wasn't, in general, feeling right.

But the operator wanted to know what was Miami like. And Tuscaloosa.

I didn't really know. I only saw the hotels and what was around the hotels.

She said, Tuscaloosa, Now that's a mouthful.

There was a nurse who came in to care for my mother.

She closed my mother's eyes and removed my mother's fingers from the edges of the bed one finger at a time with a pencil.

My brother said this on my machine.

He said, She used a fucking pencil.

Because my mother had died in her sleep, drugged, everyone called it peaceful.

But—maybe obvious to say—who can say what she was dreaming.

My father met the nurse at a convention. I imagine them talking beneath the ballroom chandelier. My father says, What's black and white and red all over. She says, What. He says, A newspaper. She doesn't get it. He says, A nun with a spear though her chest. She says, You're awful, laughing and smacks his arm. He says, A penguin who's been shot. She says, You're killing me, and covers her mouth. She's wearing white stockings. My father gets her number. She becomes his lifelong friend.

Then my mother gets sicker.

A good thing the nurse coming in to care for my mother.

A fluke the nurse becoming my father's girlfriend.

I once said to my shrink, I never went to see my mother before she died.

I said, How do you feel about that.

When my brother went, he stood by her bed.

He called me and said, It's not even her.

So why should I visit, I thought.

My brother said she ate crumbled toast. Her mouth was always open wide. She lay, curled, unmoving, on the hospital bed they had rented and set up in the living room.

Like a fucking table, my brother said.

We just sit around it, he said.

From the floor I told my shrink about my swimsuit. It didn't fit, and I feared the men would laugh.

She said, There's no time now.

She said, Can this wait until Wednesday.

It was Friday. I would see her Wednesday after work. But there were days to get through before then. And I wanted something on the phone.

I said, But my father and brother always laughed.

I now owned a beachrobe.

She said, Can it wait.

In the beginning, I went to the convention, truth be told, to look at men. To pick up men.

I cared less about the convention itself, its topic I mean, and more about picking up men in suits. I wanted something lifelong.

I drank with men in cocktail lounges at the ends of days.

But they were the dullest men, convention die-hards, and I spent most nights in my room alone, watching TV.

Once I called my brother from Kansas City. I said, Guess where I am.

He said, You're desperate for friends.

He said, You're becoming you-know-who.

In the rooms our suitcases spilled out onto the floor. My brother's model plane parts were spread about. The glue he used made my head come unhinged. It felt like being underwater.

So I suppose I should have liked this.

Underwater was no sound, no light.

Above water was a mess.

My father used to say about my mother, She can't let things go.

She couldn't let things go.

What things.

This and that.

He traveled a lot. He smelled of smoke.

But she let the big thing go, you know.

My father said this. She let the big thing go, Ha ha.

No one thought this was funny. Not even he did after he said it.

When my mother got sicker, my father called the nurse he liked the most. She kept my mother drugged as my father said to do. The drugs dripped into my mother's arm. My mother said some of the strangest things. My father called to tell me what.

He laughed and I could hear the nurse laughing in the background.

I said, What the hell's so funny.

He said, You have no sense of humor.

Perhaps this was true.

A man who had bent my ear in the ballroom with jokes approached me poolside. I was removing my terrycloth beachrobe. He said, I've got a good one.

After each joke he said, Do you get it, and poked me in the ribs.

But I didn't get it.

And each time he poked me in the ribs, I felt my ribs and what my ribs were supposed to be protecting, and the terror of this.

That ribs protect organs. Skin protects ribs. Hair protects skin. And then what.

There was a day, sitting on the edge of a bed, my father and mother and brother on the beach, the TV on, the model glue in its tiny tube just across the room.

I uncapped the glue tube and breathed in the fumes, and deeply I should say, and my head went murky, swimming in black.

I tried calling girls from back home, but I couldn't get my head to clear, so I threw several of my brother's model planes, still wet with glue and paint, through the hotel room window.

I didn't think they would fly, but I wondered how they would crash.

But to my surprise they flew.

Often the phone rang when I was in my shrink's office, and I always knew when the phone was ringing though she kept the ringer off.

I knew the phone was ringing because a red light on the phone would blink, and it made me just wild to see the light.

Often I said, Your phone is ringing.

My shrink said, Can you try to ignore it.

But I stared at the light until it stopped blinking.

I know I should at least have tried to ignore it.

But it could have been a friend or her mother or some die-hard patient desperate for who knows what.

My shrink said, What does this mean to you.

It meant something dull, like who was I and what was life.

I said, It means your phone is ringing.

I watched as my brother dumped butterflies, dead, from a plastic bag.

He pushed straight pins straight through their center parts and stuck them to a piece of board.

I suppose he should have preserved them in some way. Their wings, eventually, dropped off in powdery bits.

When my father called and said, I'm sorry, I said, What did you do.

He said, Your mother died.

He said, Where have you been.

I said, At the convention.

He said, That's my girl.

My brother and the nurse had carried my mother's body out to the lawn on the bed.

My brother called and told my machine, We put her on the

fucking lawn.

I heard him say this in real time. I was reading a magazine.

He didn't want me to know he was crying.

I read an article on weight loss. It suggested exercise and low fat foods.

My brother never liked me to know he was crying. When a wave knocked him down, he pretended the water stung his eyes.

I would laugh and run to the room. From the room I called the girls. First one then another then another.

I said, I'm calling from the beach, when there was a beach.

And they always found ways to disconnect.

And my brother would find me. And I'd call him baby. And he'd pin me to the floor.

My brother had said, It's not even her.

I said, Sometimes I'm not even me.

He said, What does that mean.

I said, I'm thinking of seeing a shrink.

He said, You're thinking of buying a friend.

But I was feeling something. Or I was feeling nothing.

This is how it starts.

One year at the convention, I met a man who seemed less dull than the others.

His suit looked less pathetic, his shoes better groomed, and we had a nice talk as we walked through the ballroom collecting things from tables into our tote bags.

We had a private dinner in the hotel, and he told me I had

quite a body, and I said nothing, looked at the table, and he laughed at something, perhaps at how I had become a girl.

Truth be told, I felt like a girl, covering my face with my hand and laughing.

His body was average, his face as well, and at some point— I'll just say it—I learned about his wife and kids.

I learned the hard way, or was it the easy way, when, in his bed, his wife called and he picked up and said, Hi honey, and, Yes baby, and pinched different sections of my skin.

Still, I stayed the night. And in the morning when I waked he was dressed and sitting on a chair reading the newspaper and I said, Hey, and he said nothing and I said, What are you doing today, and he lowered the newspaper and said, What, and I said, Today, and he said, I don't understand.

I don't know why they put my mother on the lawn.

But at least it was summer.

There was a day I ran into the field of brown grass and wildflowers, my brother's butterflies still alive in a plastic bag.

I wish I could say I let them go and that they flew far from the field so my brother could never recatch them.

Yes, I thought they would fly.

But I turned the bag over to let them go and they fell to the ground in circles, sunk in the tall brown grass and flowers.

I went home once after my mother died. I thought to visit the girls. But I didn't know where any of them lived. So many years had passed. And I never liked them, besides. And they never liked me.

When we got back from my father's convention one year, the girls had, together, ganged up on me for reasons having to do with my calling too much.

When I told my father, he said, Those bitches, and I laughed so hard I thought I would crumble to the ground.

I collected my mother's things into tote bags. There wasn't much I wanted.

My father's girlfriend lay on the couch, watching TV and smoking. She wore my mother's robe.

It wasn't a beachrobe but some other old thing my mother wore around the house.

My brother was putting things he wanted of my mother's into boxes.

It wasn't worth fighting over the things.

When my father's girlfriend stood, I noticed she was very tall and the robe stopped just above her knees.

I let her hug me.

Then I went into the field behind the house, more overgrown than ever, brown grass taller than I was.

It looked like rain, so I stayed just for a moment.

In the fitting room the salesgirl said, Let's see you.

I admit I was afraid, at first, to part the curtain. I didn't want the salesgirl looking at my body, for—and I admit this, too, hard as it is—I didn't exactly feel like the body's owner. As an owner with any sort of choice in the matter—and this isn't a joke—I believe I would have chosen another model.

But I parted the curtain.

I waited as the salesgirl looked.

My father took us to a diner in a part of town I had never seen. My brother and I rode in the back seat. The windshield wipers made a sound like something—I'll just say it—a sound like crying. At the diner I ordered toast.

The girlfriend said, Your mom was nice.

They all ordered quite a lot to eat and ate like horses.

My father told a story about something the girlfriend did. Something stupid. She stuck a fork in a plugged-in toaster. Or she dropped the phone into the tub. Or she left the iron face-down, hot, on the ironing board. He pretended to be angry when she didn't laugh. The girlfriend smacked him on the arm and called him awful.

He told her she needed new dresses.

He said, She'll send me to the poorhouse yet.

I can't explain why this bothers me still. I mean, the girlfriend's gone. The day he threw her out of the house, my father called and told my machine, I threw the bitch out.

The man at the pool held my arm. He said, I've got a good one.

He said, This girl, see, is walking through a field…

Okay.

And she's lost and scared, so she keeps on walking and, lucky for her, she sees a house with lights on, so she knocks on the door

of the house and a man answers, and she says, I'm hoping you can
help…

Okay.

So the man says to the girl, I'd love to help you out, and in-
vites her inside and says she can spend the night at his house and
promises he'll take her home in the morning if she…

Stop, I said.

He said, What.

I covered my ears.

Just stop, I said.

I sat in the waiting room with a magazine. A girl waited, too,
on a chair near mine. She looked at me. I must have been looking
at her.

I read an article on how to be more assertive. It suggested a
firm handshake, eye to eye.

I heard my shrink open her door down the hall. I felt ready
to talk.

First of my father throwing his girlfriend out. We would
laugh our heads off over that.

And there was still the matter of my swimsuit.

And the matter, too, of the beachrobe.

My shrink came into the waiting room. I stood and said hello.
This always made me feel like a kid. Like a shy kid hiding behind
my mother's legs in a crowd.

The girl stood, too, and said hello.

My shrink said my name.

She said, Come with me.

We walked partway down the hall to her office.

She said, It's Tuesday.

She said, You're Wednesday.

She said, I'll see you tomorrow.

She walked me back to the waiting room.

She said to the girl waiting, I'm sorry.

The girl looked at me and went with my shrink down the hall.

She was taller than I was. Better looking.

I didn't return to see my shrink. I was tired of talking. And she would send me to the poorhouse, besides.

My father and brother once managed to pinch.

My mother laughed as I stood on the sand.

The ocean meant me and the fishes.

The hotel room meant me on the phone.

And I just stood there, frozen.

My mother said, Just tell her you're sorry.

My brother ran into the ocean.

My father said, What's got two hands and flies.

It hurt where he pinched. So I ran to the room. No, I kept on running. There was a mall nearby, and I ran into the mall in my swimsuit. I was barefoot. It was freezing in there.

I could have sunk into the field behind the house, the field just wild with tall brown grass.

The air smelled like rain. I looked at the house's black windows.

I imagined the poorhouse as looking like our house.

I once said to my shrink, How do you feel about that.

My shrink said, I feel with my hands, Ha ha.

There was a night I watched my mother fall asleep sitting up on the hotel bed, her mouth wide open, the TV flashing on her gray face. And I poked her in the arm to wake her, and she didn't move, and I poked her in the ribs, and I jumped on the bed screaming, Wake up, and my brother, building a plane on the floor, looked up, said, Quit it, and I said, Baby, and he said, I'll kill you, and went back to his plane. And I jumped on the bed wildly, screaming, Wake up, Wake up, until my father walked in, smelling of smoke and drinks and perfume and who knows what else and said, Don't jump on the bed, and my mother waked and said, Where have you been, and reached for the pen on the table beside the bed and threw the pen at my father.

I started to say to the operator, I'm disconnecting, but instead I said, I've got a good one.

This girl's walking along the beach and she's thinking...

My shrink's machine picked up.

The operator said, I'm sorry.

How she works in an office doing who knows what...

The operator said, Machine.

She disconnected.

So this girl's running along the road, and she's running from her father who has just pinched her in a place I can't divulge, and she's running from her brother who has also just pinched her and now laughs his head off in the shallowest part of the ocean, and she's running from her mother who looks gray and sick and no one's doing a damn thing about it because no one knows for sure what's wrong, and she sees a mall and decides to run inside, and there's a store in the mall that sells women's clothing, large, warm sweaters and such, and the girl, who's wearing a swimsuit—did I forget to say this—two piece, blue—and is freezing and wants nothing more at this point than to feel warm, runs into the clothing store, and a man says, Can I help you, and she says, No, and pushes her body through the tightly packed clothing hanging on a round rack and sits within the rack, yes, like in a cave, shivering, warming, imagining her mother's face, flushed, alive, in the crowd in the mall screaming her name, and the man says...

The joke ends.

I removed my beachrobe by the pool and dropped it to a chair.

The men in the pool turned to look at me.

They looked close, as if looking through holes in walls, their hands underwater, moving fast like fishes.

I said, What do you want, though I knew what they wanted.

God, who prepares one for moments like these.

The swimsuit felt like a cage.

And you want to know what the men said back.

Look. They said nothing. They turned away. They treaded water.

It wasn't lifelong, what they wanted.

So it wasn't me that they wanted.

I threw the chair into the pool. The beachrobe too. I watched them sink.

I can still hear how the men carried on.

How pathetic it was.

The men's heads bobbing in the deep end, laughing.

Gray light filtering in from winter.

Hydroplane

And several times I looked to the roadside and saw what I thought was an animal, curled, shredded, dead, but was only a pile of straw.

And this was several times of looking at a single pile on the roadside, bright in the headlights, thinking, Don't look, thinking of guts, blood smeared on the road, bits of bone and matted fur.

And every time, when I got nearer the pile and looked, after thinking, Don't, but looked because I couldn't help looking, I found this dead shredded thing was straw piled on the roadside.

I'll mention the road signs that looked like men. Wide-shouldered men on short, splayed legs.

I'll mention the tractors, how they looked like horses, how

they looked like houses, hulking on the roadside, bright in the headlights.

What all this means: it was late, dark.

What it really means: look, I can't break it down far enough to even say what straw was before it was straw.

I'll say hay.

It doesn't matter.

What matters is the road was wet for miles from rain. What matters is the tires skidded. A tire blew. The car swerved into a shallow ditch past the shoulder. And a man pulled over to help.

But before this.

What I thought: If straw looks like dead things, I need to sleep.

I thought to pull off to the shoulder.

But I kept on driving as I couldn't stop. There was a power behind this driving and driving. I had a power. It felt like that. Like something holy. Or something soaring. Predictable even. A rocket soaring through space.

And there were crazy thoughts. The likes of which I can't explain. But look, they were crazy. Somewhat psychic.

I saw the rain stop before it stopped. I saw the car skid before it skidded. The tire blew before it blew. Bits of black rubber flew up from the road. I didn't see the bits of black rubber. But I smelled the scorch.

The car stopped in a shallow ditch.

And there I was standing, waiting for help, in that nighttime cow smell, alone.

We were told in drivers' ed to wait for a man. We were told to light a flare and wait for a man to show and help with the car.

But I didn't have flares. I never have. I have never even considered flares or the heavy blanket we were told in drivers' ed to buy and keep in the trunk for reasons then unknown.

I was driving across from Baltimore. And if a tire blows in Baltimore, there's a place to ditch the car and a bus to take home if one has the fare.

I was driving across to teach.

I stand in a classroom most days.

I stand there thinking, How am I here.

I think, Out the window, Look how flat.

It's Missouri out there is what I think. That somehow I got to Missouri.

I stopped out front of my mother's house before I went.

My mother was standing on the walk.

I rolled down the window and waved.

My mother said, Pull over.

She said, Come on.

I pulled over but didn't get out of the car.

My cat slept in a box on the seat.

My mother said, You and that dirty cat.

She said, Why Missouri.

Good question.

I imagined flat and endless farms.

And imagine. It was all I imagined.

To live, I said.

To make a living, I said.

You and your living, my mother said.

We shook hands through the window before I went.

Then the ride. The ride's euphoric moments. A song I knew. The sunrise in the rearview mirror. Predictable thoughts of what if what if what if.

Dumb.

He kissed my nose, and I will always say he didn't mean to. His aim was off. I will always say it.

Look, I hadn't thought of him of flares of blankets since

drivers' ed, and that was high school, that was summers ago in the church basement, the teacher with the stained shirts and glass eye. What did we call him. I don't know. The boys all called him something. His eye like some kind of milky jewel rolling back and forth in its socket. His gut pushing out the sauce stains on his shirts. And his son who took us on the road in the long red car with the zigzag stripe and the brake on the passenger's side. The boys all talked about the long red car, even that boy with the off aim.

It's fast, said the boy one night behind the headstone.

But it wasn't fast, as it turned out. Sure it looked fast with the zigzag stripe. But the boy hadn't driven the long red car. He didn't know how slow it went. I was first to drive it in the class. I didn't want to drive it first. But the teacher said my name. He was not a Jew. This my mother told me. He had a good last name my mother said. He said mine wrong. He said, You're first, and everyone laughed at the thought.

When I went driving with the teacher's son, the car went so slow, the teacher's son said, Are you on pills, as if it were my fault how we crept. And I said to him, Your car has no power.

He said something back I can't remember. Something I can't quite care about now.

And had I told my mother what he said.

She would have held my hand.

She would have said, Fix your nails.

She would have said, You won't get married with nails like those.

I sat in the graveyard behind the church at night with the boys from drivers' ed. It was dark and quiet but for us. Just one boy worth mentioning today. Just that boy I already mentioned. Just one night worth mentioning in the graveyard. I gave that boy two pills that night, pressed them into his palm, and he showed them to the other boys. He said, I told you she wants me.

I said, I don't like you.

Then a scuffle. Me and the boy scuffling in the grass. The other boys running off for good. Me and the boy sitting in the grass.

The moon shone on the backs of headstones.

Crosses stuck up from their tops.

We were sitting in the grass when the cops came prowling.

But this isn't about him and me sitting in the grass. And this isn't about those Baltimore cops with nothing better to do but prowl.

This is about Missouri.

Imagine this place. There are no streetlights. The road is wet with rain.

And at some point my tire will blow. The car will skid and stop in a ditch. I will get out of the car and stand in a pile of straw with the cat. I will wait for a man. He will pull over. He will help me change the tire. He will drive the car from the ditch to the shoulder. Then he will touch me in the wet straw.

The drivers' ed teacher told us girls to learn to change a tire. He said, In case a man doesn't pull over. He said, Ask your fathers to show you how.

I asked my mother how to change a tire.

She said, Ask who you marry to do it for you.

She said, You'll marry if you fix your nails.

I was arrested in the graveyard that night. The boy was arrested. I'd say the cops were pushy that night. They said things to me I can't remember. Though I do remember the boy laughed hard. The cops laughed too.

They pushed me into one car, the boy into another.

I can't care about what they said.

And besides. It doesn't matter. None of it does. In Missouri everything changed.

I was standing in straw with the cat. I was waiting for something. I don't know what. A man I thought.

Early, I had driven toward a sunset. A song came on. And the night felt holy, as I mentioned, somehow. Then more so as the sky turned black. I soared like a rocket through the dark. The road was wet. It was black everywhere the headlights weren't. The headlights hit the straw and again. I was looking at all that straw thinking, Come on already, Happen already. I knew something would. And then the car skidded. The wheel turned on its own. I recall the dark thrill of a hydroplane. We had learned of these in drivers' ed. The road was wet enough to skid on. Perhaps it was then the tire blew. What did they teach us of hydroplaning. To turn the wheel to the shoulder. I remembered. I veered the car toward the shoulder and the car stopped past in a ditch.

I was stuck.

First thought: It's quiet.

Then: I have no flares.

And, as mentioned, I had never even considered flares. And if I'd had them, I would never have lighted them on the roadside for various reasons, one having to do with a fear of the straw catching fire and then, in time, of farmland Missouri going up in flames.

But the straw was wet and wouldn't catch fire. I knew this. It was too wet.

Regardless.

I wouldn't have wanted cops to see flares and find me there stuck in a ditch. Because I knew how cops could get when a girl made a dumb mistake.

My mistake was not checking the tires before I went. There was a way to check. A way to kick.

My mistake that one night was not ducking lower in the grass. We should have ducked low, me and the boy. I should have ducked my head to his lap. He should have lowered his head to my shoulder. But he kissed my nose, this boy, behind the headstone, and it felt like something, his kiss. Sandpaper. Predictable.

The cops came prowling through the graveyard with flashlights, with nothing better to do but prowl, and saw our heads above the headstone.

They said, Look at this.

We didn't jump.

We weren't scared.

Our legs touched in the grass.

When drivers' ed ended, the boys went driving. They drove their fathers' cars. I drove a car my mother bought. The boys didn't want to ride with me. The boys stopped going to the graveyard. They all thought I was too good now. This, because I owned a car. The teacher's son owned two. The boys had told me this. That he owned two. They told me one night in the graveyard. Our first night there. Nothing worth mentioning now. A night I told them I could get pills. I said, I can give you what you want. We sat and talked, big deal. We talked about getting high. We sat in a circle, and I said, I can get you pills.

The boys said the teacher's son had a sports car.

Well, then, I would see this car. I would tell the boys about it. I would tell the boy I wanted.

I said, Next week, I'll get you high.

The boys said the teacher's son lived in a house.

I would see the house, then, too.

The teacher's son had a mustache.

When he picked me up in his long red car, my mother wasn't yet home from work. He knocked. I wanted to call out, Later Ma, before leaving the house, but she was still at work.

And so I drove his car through Baltimore. It felt vast and light, like pushing a weightless building up the streets. And now I can say it was euphoric, pushing this thing. I have not felt anything like it since.

Look, I was laughing so hard, pushing slow and loose and light through the streets, that the teacher's son said, Are you on pills.

It doesn't matter that he said this.

I knew better than to drive on pills.

And yes his car had a type of power despite what I said.

Regardless.

What matters is what happened later.

I was stranded on the roadside in farmland Missouri. I was stuck there standing in straw like a cow.

What matters is the car that eventually came.

I didn't wave down the car.

I stood there waiting as if waiting for nothing.

I thought of my mother as I stood there. I thought of what she would have done. She would have waved down this car with her fixed up nails, screaming, Stop.

Her rings would have glinted in the headlights.

She would have said to me, Straighten, as the man stepped from his car.

She often said, Straighten.

She often said, They want one thing, Give them what they want.

She often said, Here's five dollars, Fix your nails.

I always took the five dollars. I bought small white pills with the money.

Because no one was looking at my nails.

I should have said, Ma, they're looking at my tits, You know this.

They weren't huge.

But I saw how the teacher's son looked when I drove.

He said, Can you change a flat tire.

We were drifting past rows of small houses.

He said, I can teach you.

He said, Pull over.

We were drifting outside a small house, and he said, I live in this house. He said, Let's change a tire together.

It was his house, not his father's. He lived in his own house because he was old enough to live alone. And he had the thick mustache of a man, not sprigs of hair that felt like sandpaper on my face. He said, Pull over, and I let the car drift toward a tree. It felt so easy and lightweight drifting. He pressed the passenger brake for me when I didn't brake. He said, You're really something. He reached over and put the car into park.

He said, Come on.

And I thought, split second, Don't.

I thought, So you will never know how to change a tire. I thought, Big deal, Make him drive you home.

But I went in the house.

Because the boy would want to hear of his other car. His sports car. And the boy would want to hear of his house. And I wanted that boy. So I went.

But look. I never told the boy a thing. I never had to. And still, we sat in the graveyard that night. What does this mean. That he wanted me, this boy. It didn't matter, the teacher's son's house. It didn't matter what I saw.

Still, I got him in a way. The boy that is.

Still, we were in the graveyard that one night just doing nothing, a kiss.

Big deal the cops found us, our heads sticking up from the headstone. Big deal they pushed me into the back of a car. They pushed him into another.

In a small room, it was me and a cop. He shook a bag in front of my face.

He said, Are these your pills.

He said, Then whose are they.

I wasn't on them anyway at the time.

He said, Where did they come from.

My mother walked in.

He said, Come on.

I said, Ma.

The cops said things. They called me things. I can't care about this.

My mother's face was all unfixed. She said, You're high.

I wasn't high. But I should have been. I had almost swallowed a pill. I was sitting in the grass with the boy. The bag was open in my lap. I was holding a small white pill. The boy was holding two. We were working up spit enough to swallow.

His leg touched mine in the grass.

To this day I have not wanted anyone more.

And now. Big deal I'm grown.

I teach in Missouri. Outside the window is flat.

But look. First it's dark. I'm stuck in a ditch. A car stops up on the shoulder. The other car is not a car but a truck. No one gets out. The truck is still running. I'm standing in all that scratchy straw. The cat is standing beside me. Here's what I first think: It's a man in the truck. And then: He will help me. And then: He will touch me. His nose will come nearer mine. His teeth. Then a kiss, a taste of something old. A taste of straw even, old and hard and covered in all that Missouri dirt. Then straw against my back, cutting into my back.

He opens the door to his truck.

He wears a hat.

He says, What's your name.

I lie because I'm a Jew.

My mother told me to always lie.

My mother said, There are no Jews in Missouri.

She said, They will treat you there like you're a Jew.

The teacher laughed every time he got my name wrong and the boys in class laughed too and I always laughed. Big deal my name. They called the teacher Glass-eye. It was Glass-eye they called him, okay. Big deal what they called me, laughing. Big deal the boy laughed too. I didn't care that he laughed. I cared about getting his face to press against mine and more. But he never tried anything on me except that one night against the headstone. And it was nothing that time.

Then why am I still thinking about it.

Good question.

Because we got arrested. Before it could turn into something more.

Before his mouth went lower.

Before my hands went to his hair.

The cops said, Look at this.

His hand was on my face.

I can't remember what I said.

Perhaps there was nothing for me to say.

Sometimes there was nothing.

When we went driving the teacher's son said, Are you on pills. And what was there for me to say. I was just euphoric. I couldn't press the brake I was so euphoric from drifting in that car. He had to press the brake for me. He put the car into park. We were near pressed to a tree out front of his house. He laughed at me. And when he laughed, I noticed lines around his eyes and that he looked older than he should have looked. I followed him into the house. He gave me a can of soda in the kitchen. He opened the can. He said, I'll be back. He went into the bathroom. I didn't drink the soda. There was a calendar on the wall. It had pictures of naked girls on it. Their tits were huge. He came into the kitchen and said, Come into the garage. He said that was where the other car was. The sports car the boys had talked about. It had a flat. He'd show me how to change a tire.

Looking back I realize I should have called my mother at work from his house. There was a telephone next to the calendar. I would have said where I was. I would have said, I'm at the drivers' ed teacher's son's house, Ma.

But this would have made no difference. He had a good last name, this one. My mother would have said so. Give him what he wants, she would have said. He had a good last name I can't remember. And a first name I also can't remember. The boys called him by his first name. The boys called his father Glass-eye.

And Glass-eye called me something. His son did too. The cops did too. The boys.

They called me Princess.

No. That wasn't it.

Yes. Because I was a Jew.

No. Something else. For another reason.

Now, really, though, this means nothing.

None of it's worth breaking down.

And straw was once hay, I'll guess. And hay was once grass.

It doesn't matter.

What matters is I was standing in straw with the cat. And look. When the teacher told us to keep a blanket in the trunk of the car, I didn't know what for. But on the roadside, I thought, A blanket, I'm supposed to have a blanket. I thought, Perhaps this man, if I had a blanket, would touch me on the blanket instead of in all this straw.

I was on my way to a school. I was a teacher.

I am a teacher. It's my living.

I stand in the front of a classroom.

I stand there talking to a hundred looking eyes.

And sometimes I'll be talking, and I'll look around the classroom, and something, perhaps a student, perhaps a boy in the
back of the room, someone who spits tobacco into a cup when I
am talking, someone who never says a word in class but sits there,
rather, staring at me, will remind me of the man on the roadside.

He said, Looks like you shredded it good.

He said, I can help.

He came nearer.

The teacher never said to carry mace. But I thought of
it once in the church basement. We were watching films of car
wrecks. I couldn't look at the wreckage. I stared instead at the pitiful stain on the teacher's shirt, thinking how it looked like blood,
thinking how his gut stretched the stain into cloud shapes, how
pitiful it was. I was thinking how it could pin me down, that gut. I
was so high that night I thought his gut was stretching toward me
to get me and pin me down. And so I stared instead at that milky
eye thinking, Fall out of the socket, Fall out of the socket, Roll onto
the table. But it stayed stuck in the socket. And I thought of mace.
I thought of how mace wouldn't hurt his eye. I knew it would just
coat the eye like any other thing, like a spray of spit, that I would
need to spray mace into the other eye to make the eye sting. I
would need good aim.

Then the teacher couldn't touch me.

And his son with two good eyes stinging from mace couldn't
touch me.

Regardless. I was high and thinking dumb.

The wrecks went on and on.

And his son and I really did change a tire. We did. It was flat,
this tire. Nearly shredded. I helped him jack up the car. Every one
of my nails had black under it after touching the greasy jack. He
said, Listen. He twisted some metal thing around some other metal
things. He had names for the parts, but I wasn't really listening.

And he was mumbling. He wasn't really saying what he was doing. He was looking at my tits from below me. He was making jokes I didn't get.

He said, Are you Jew.

He said, You know what they say about Jew girls.

But I didn't know, and I still don't. And it never occurred to me to leave his house. I could have left. I wasn't locked in. It was Baltimore and I knew how to get home. There was a bus to take. It went from his corner to mine. I knew where I was. He was on the floor partway under the car. I was standing by him. He could have touched my legs with his face. I could feel him breathing on my legs. But he wasn't holding me there. I wasn't stuck. Look. I went into the bathroom. I looked in the mirror. I fixed up my lipstick. There was a towel on the floor. A smell of cologne. A stain in the bathtub. I cupped water from the sink in my hand and drank. I was beautiful in that bathroom mirror. Do you understand this. I was something else. There was my soda on the kitchen table. The calendar girls with the huge tits. It never occurred to me to leave his house. He called my name from the garage. He said it correctly. I said, I'm coming. It never occurred to me to leave his house, until I was walking home later with my shirt on inside-out. It was night.

My mother said, Would you look at this.

And this is what's funny. That now I'm a teacher. That I teach, that is. That I say how it goes. That all those eyes are looking at my eyes looking at the flat past the window.

They want me to tell them something true.

So this is what's true.

So this man on the roadside is true.

I can't say exactly what he looked like. He was big, I recall. Old, I suppose. His teeth looked rotted. But it was dark. He wore a cross on a chain around his neck. It swung when he leaned in toward me. He wore a hat. He changed my tire. He moved my car to the shoulder. He smoked the whole time. He was breathing hard. He said, Let's go for a ride.

I said, I'm a teacher.

He said, I'll be your student.

He laughed and I thought of his laugh against all that farm-land quiet.

And I didn't really get the joke.

I thought, split second, to say, Explain.

When the teacher's son said, You know about Jew girls, I said, What about them.

He said, I like you.

I knew he did. I knew when someone liked me.

We were lying on the greasy floor. I saw light through the garage door windows. The light was white, then red. His mustache scratched my face. When I screamed it scared him. He jumped up saying, What the fuck. He said, Go home.

Tell me why this matters.

Since then there have been many men.

My mother said, You could have been beautiful, You could have been married.

She said, You could have been something else.

We shook hands through the window before I went. I felt her nails, her rings, pressing into my palm.

There was a time I liked her.

When I was young, a kid, my mother would pull my hair, and I would say, Hey, stop that, Ma, and she would say, Hay is for horses, Hay is for horses, and I would say back, Hay is for horses, and she would clap and I would clap, and boy did we laugh our heads off.

Though I don't understand why it made us laugh.

Look.

This man in Missouri was big. He could have crushed me.

Really. His gut. His shoulders. We were standing in the straw. There was no moon. I had no mace. He could have crushed me to bits.

My cat ran into the car.

The man stood near, his cross swinging against his chest, then not.

He smelled like smoke.

He could have crushed me to bits.

But I can't take this a step further.

I can't keep pretending he touched me. He didn't.

I wasn't psychic.

Though he could have touched me. You know he could have as he was so big and I was not.

But this is how it goes.

I said something like, I like your cross.

He touched his cross.

He said something, nothing important, and left.

But this isn't about him either. Look. What matters is I made it to where I was going.

And sometimes I'm on the couch at home in Missouri. And sometimes I find myself thinking on the couch about that night. I think about what could have happened. But the man drives off and I'm lying on a greasy floor. And it's me and the teacher's son lying there. He says, Look at you, and he sends his fingers up inside, first one, then two, without any warning, without ever asking, and the light turns red and I scream, Stop, and he presses his mouth to mine and hard and I try to scream and I push him off of me and scream, Stop it, and he screams at me and sends me home.

And I think of my mother saying, as I opened the door that night crying, Would you look at this, Your shirt's on inside-out, you slob.

And I remember the boys, how they looked at me laughing, and I remember what they called me after they went with the teacher's son on the road in the long red car, after the teacher's son said what to call me.

And I watch my cat cleaning his paws at one end of the couch, wondering at the length of his tongue, wondering how his tongue keeps him clean.

There was a night alone in the graveyard. It was late that summer, almost fall. I swallowed a pill, sat in the grass. The boys all thought I was something now. Dried flowers poked up from the dirt. The boys all thought I was too bad now. The moon was higher than the top of the church. The moon was rising higher. The boys all thought I was too loose now. I was too fast now. But really I was something else. I looked for signs of our having been there. A hair in the grass from when we were there. A dropped pill. A thread. But it was dark. And I was scared. And there was nothing of ours in the grass.

The pill put clouds behind my forehead.

Big deal, I drove home high.

It was loose, light, fast.

Euphoric.

And you know this is what matters.

And now I'm in the mirror at home. I'm on my way to teach. I've got a pitiful sauce stain on my shirt, and I think, You better scrub out that stain before you teach. And the telephone rings, and mail gets pushed through the slot. The cat needs to eat. I'm running to get there on time.

Well, I get to school, and the sauce stain is still on my shirt.

I'm standing in front of a class.

A hundred eyes are looking at me.

A boy spits tobacco into a cup.

But what matters is you're with me now.

I've got you where I want you.

This is the happy ending.

A man changed my tire. He drove my car to the shoulder. He said something. Nothing. The man drove off. I drove off. There was a song I knew. A sunrise in the rearview mirror. Me and the boy fucking in the grass.